From

The Women's Press Ltd
in association with Hutchinson Group (NZ) Ltd

Janet Frame was born in Dunedin, New Zealand, in 1924. She studied at Dunedin Teachers' Training College and the University of Otago but left teaching after one year to concentrate on her writing. Her first book was a collection of short stories called *The Lagoon* which she wrote when she was 21 and was working as a housemaid in Dunedin.

Her work since that time includes ten novels, among them *Owls Do Cry*, *A State of Siege*, *Scented Gardens for the Blind*, *Yellow Flowers in the Antipodean Room* and *Faces in the Water*, which is also available from The Women's Press; also four collections of stories and sketches, a volume of poetry and a children's book, *Mona Minim and the Smell of the Sun*.

Janet Frame has been a Burns Scholar, has won the New Zealand Scholarship in letters, the Hubert Church Award for New Zealand prose and, in 1979, was awarded an honorary Doctor of Literature degree by the University of Otago.

Janet Frame now lives in Wanganui, New Zealand.

About Janet Frame
'A passionate devotion to the idiosyncratic prerogatives of art...Frame's writing has an arresting flavour that is not to be obtained from anyone else' *The Washington Star*

'With each new novel since the publication of her first, *Owls Do Cry*, in 1960, Janet Frame has won praise as New Zealand's leading woman novelist...Frame's inventive lyrical prose will continue to delight those who read for more than a story' *Library Journal*

'Like the late Jean Rhys, this remarkable New Zealand novelist has built up a literary reputation that fair dazzles, and deservedly so' *Publishers Weekly*

"Those creatures and worlds that we know only in sleep and dream and mythology—of yesterday and of today—the magical technology — are emerging as usual reality in the new dimension of living and dying. And when the unreal has been accepted and made real, new realities will present themselves, forces which become gentlenesses, gentlenesses which become forces."

"A pretty theory."

Brian, whose pursuit of an idea was direct and always victorious, whose intellectual power was more certain than mine, was inclined to disperse my cloudy thought with a keen icy breeze of logic.

"Just suppose Tommy was really overtaken by this Blue Fury —"

"But we saw it; or rather we saw him disappear—"

"By your theory he still exists, he's merely returned beneath the surface of apparent reality . . . ."

We gave up talking of the incident. I went upstairs and took Tommy's world-earrings and starfish brooch out of my purse and studied them, hoping for a sign. Then I thrust them to the bottom of my suitcase. I spent a restless night. Sounds from the street and the alley: laughter, shouts; police and traffic sirens; gunshots; the fear as a car stopped, silently, secretively, outside the window. I kept a light burning at half-glow on the big old dresser that Brian had bought, with his other furniture, from the Salvation Army store.

The next day, although I didn't tell Brian, I telephoned the upstairs apartment where Tommy lived (Brian had the number in case of emergency) and asked to speak to Tommy. The owner obligingly went down to fetch him and returned to say that he had gone, his door was wide open, his room was cleaned out and there was no sign of him.

"You a friend of his?"

"A friend of a friend."

"I tell you one thing. There's a necklace, a string of small globes, looks like worlds. Cute, like cages. And there's a dead bird in a birdcage."

I thanked him and hung up. I was surprised. I didn't remember a bird, living or dead, only the wide-open cage with the To Let sign, hanging from the ceiling.

Brian and I kept our word and didn't mention Tommy again. He slipped out of our lives, as people do, their only legacy being the first three words of a sentence spoken or written, "Whatever happened to . . ."

I returned to Blenheim to continue my writing career, and I didn't think again of the Blue Fury until my next husband died. For you see, for reasons inexplicable now— yet why should I explain, I am not in California!—I married Lance Halleton, the French teacher at the local girls' school.

7.

I had known Lance Halleton when his wife was alive and my daughter Edith was in his class at school. I'd been impressed by his teaching and by his apparent devotion to the French language, and when his wife died (within months of Lewis's death), we shared the experience of being the conspicuous bereaved, the two strangers who find they both speak the same language. We both resented this, but when I returned to Blenheim I found that I was spending some time with my writing and the rest of the time being susceptible to Lance's passion for the French language. I've always admired enthusiasts who become lost in their enthusiasm and I soon found out what happens when I mix my admiration with a little sympathy, pity, sense of adventure, loneliness, desire for love and to be loved, in a mixing-bowl of a city, where the streets are named after battles with never a sign of who lost or who won or how many died, and certainly, though the generals were named, no names of any of the warriors. The streets tell the names of the battles, but it is literature and our imagination which tells us about those who fought.

It was after an evening spent with Lance Halleton when he read to me in French Victor Hugo's *Retreat from Moscow* that we decided to marry. I should have been concerned when Lance slept on our wedding night with two pocket calculators under his pillow!

Three weeks after our marriage he resigned from teaching to become a debt collector.

We had decided to live in my old home in Bannockburn Road. He measured the house, carefully working out in both imperial and metric measure the volume of each room, the amount of space each would need and the number of BTU's necessary to gives us our required warmth — an activity to be commended in a new husband anxious to satisfy the ordinary human needs of his wife and himself and healthily curious about all kinds of space — outer, inner, nearer — that which rests on the skin and before the eyes and can be reached at little or no cost.

It was the *cost* of all things, including the cost of living which now worried Lance: the cost of living, the national debt, who would pay, what was being paid for and how could one know when it was finally paid? One might say it was a cruel act of fate for a man like Lance, his life built of French verbs in their tenses and moods, safely fattened by his never having traveled out of New Zealand, to be confronted now by the national debt. People might have said that he was mad, that it was his age and the age he lived in, that a person of middle age, whether married or single, stands suddenly upon a bare plain and will be blown by whatever wind passes by; that it is glacier-time too, the time for the splinter of ice in the eye, the distortion of vision, impulsive matings, journeys toward that are believed to be journeys away from, and journeys away that are really journeys within. A lifetime even of French verbs is no shelter for that middle-age landscape and weather, nor is a first marriage, nor a sudden change of occupation.

I learned that Lance had already found a job with a debt-collecting firm.

"This very city," he said, "is full of people who don't or won't or can't pay. Blenheim is an ideal place for me to work. My boss thinks so too."

I, who supposed I knew something of Lance's character,

was astonished by the urgency, the vindictiveness of his statement. Surely it was "out of character" for Lance, the French teacher, the man I had just married—although to be "out of character," you must first be "in character," and as I thought about this I realized that perhaps Lance had never been thus. As a teacher of French he had really been a speckled sort of man, a kindly hen of no fixed sex; sensitive, with a well-lubricated voice with a resonance that made him a fine speaker and reader of poetry. He blushed easily, and had quickly aroused sympathy in his students, and in me. I confess that he was the kind of man that I used to say I despised (this feeling as a legacy from the setting of those sharply defined always fashionable preferences of adolescence) yet face to face with him I loved him because he had an abiding passion for the French language. The apparent purity and vastness of his feeling gave him, in my eyes, a kind of greatness, for I feel that language in its widest sense is the hawk suspended above eternity, feeding from it but not of its substance and not necessarily for its life and thus never able to be translated into it; only able by a wing movement, so to speak, a cry, a shadow, to hint at what lies beneath it on the untouched, undescribed almost unknown plain.

There was an innocence about Lance. I marvelled at his knowledge of places he had never visited except in his imagination, and yet there was a suggestion of his being an exile even from there, and a loneliness which endeared him to me although I'm not sure that in marrying him my intention was to keep or break that innocence. I know he was the last person on earth to become a debt collector, and perhaps that was why he was given the job when others, including expolicemen, were unsuccessful. His obsessive interest in debt and its payment combined with his persuasive voice, which in the past could move at a breath from subjunctive to dative to imperative to copulative mood, apparently convinced the firm that employing him would result in the payment of the many bad debts lurking behind the venetian blinds and ranch-sliders of Blenheim.

I tried to analyze "my" Lance. I had "done" psychology years ago as a student, but I soon gave up trying to find early experiences that would be responsible for his obsession, and of course I did not want to blame recent experiences (I was aware that my first husband, also, had switched his vocation: medical student to drain-layer). Our former lives had become finished games and closed books and sometimes when we spoke of them or were reminded of them by chance meetings or items of news or photographs, our conversation was like that of tourists who visited the same country years ago before everything was demolished, changed, developed. Memory Country: bathed in cloud and light; where the planes and ships rarely call now.

I decided that it was Lance's "age" which determined his sudden change (just as I had decided it was my "age" which caused my romantic attachment to him to crystallize in marriage, particularly as I had set my heart on a writing career, although this dream, too, was infected with reality — those successful women writers who maintain a home and family life and, attended by servants real or imaginary, still write). In the end I felt that Lance was merely trapped in his own store of guilt. *He* wanted to pay. He was in the mood which sees the stirring of religion where debt is important enough to be mentioned in daily prayers and although it is the forgiveness which is stressed and granted, the fact of the debt is there. You have been given, you have bought, you have stolen, and you *owe*, even from before your very first breath. Life on earth is so arranged that you may be granted each day, day after day, for a lifetime, and avoid making payment — a secondary avoidance. The primary avoidance is in being unable to see that the desire to pay is essentially one untroubled by petty calculations and is not even dependent upon having been given, having received, bought, or stolen. It is in not recognizing that in a world of replicas the original cannot be matched in value, and the real fact is often a copy of the unreal fiction, and perpetual human joy and suffering lie in the yearning, not only to pay, but to identify the original as itself apart, not as real or unreal or as opposite or adjacent; paying for it in the sense that the blossoms pay for the spring by flourishing within it as part of it.

As I, too, was of an age when avoidances may become inexcusable and ridiculous, I fancied that I could identify the origin of the feeling which obsessed Lance. I called it the *Hypotenuse longing*. Geometry and payments are a relic of my school days, indeed of my first week at school when a teacher suddenly shouted at me, "Pay attention! Come out here!"

I came "out there."

She strapped my hand with a leather strap, and said sternly, "In future, pay attention."

I now see attention as presence, being present, as the payment for the dark debt of absence or death. Or as a response to the Hypotenuse longing.

On the days, however, when I was not feeling metaphysical I decided that Lance was suffering from financial patriotism, a natural symptom in a country where the body politic wore paper-money clothes and had kowhai gold in its two-cent eyes.

"Blenheim is our special problem," Lance's boss, Rob Guthrie, said one afternoon when he called on us. He was over six feet tall, large but not fat, and he wore the debt collectors' uniform (white bowling hat, gym shoes, shorts, a striped blazer) which put him in the company of bowlers, hunters, dart players, and fly-fishermen (Rob Guthrie had a fishing-fly, Red-Tipped-Governor stuck in his panama hat). Debt collecting, then, was a sport.

Guthrie, an expoliceman, said he had "contacts" to give him information about bad debtors. He supervised all allotted territories with special responsibility for Auckland city.

45

The problem with Blenheim was the number of people who "flitted" when they were expected to Stay, Sit, like dogs, but where the earlier generations had space and peace to Stay, Sit, Sleep, the new generation often found they had moved to Nowheresville, a desert governed from Suicide City.

I remember that day when Rob Guthrie called on us. There was a cold wind blowing in from the sea, merging familiarly with the rush hour fumes in Bannockburn Road and the last belch of the day from the factories down in Kaka Valley. Neighbors had their end of autumn fires burning and these were not fires of leaves favored by poets, but the burning of rubber tires, old carpets, and plastic containers which filled the air with a dark foul smoke. In the midst of all this burning, and as an accompaniment to it, Rob Guthrie appeared at the door—a comic figure, a joking devil in his shorts with his knees and shins carboned with blue from the first seasonal weatherprint of what, in an officially frost-free district, must be called a masquerade, an imitation of frost. I shivered at the sight of him and I couldn't bear to think that Lance would come to resemble him as a fellow sportsman, camouflaged, waiting to stalk the kill, separated from that warm intellectual house built so patiently verb by verb, conjunction interior, mood-sliders, tea terrace of adjectives, all comforts.

And that evening, as if announcing that we had received a priceless gift, Lance said, his voice joyous, "He's given me charge of the Wynyard file! He brought it to me himself! He said I can work with it in the field. Funny, he made it sound like a battlefield!"

As Lance's trusted, prudent wife I was allowed to study the file of Blenheim's chief professional debtor who was also a professional tenant, flitter by moonlight, small-time conman, who, after having worked at his specialties in other parts of New Zealand, had spent the past year or two on the North Shore, in Blenheim, where the many once bushclad

46

valleys, now housing estates, were as isolated one from the other as if they were separated by mountains instead of by the tar-sealed ridge roads all leading to the heart of the district, that broad hilltop easily recognized from a distance by its huge concrete warehouse that, as the distance succumbed to the tiled and tiny-treed nearness, became, of course, Heavenfield Mall with its golden birds brazenly singing in or out of tune with the shopper's soothing music playing from the loud-speakers fitted under what might be called for want of a term which would not promote an architectural and ornithological argument — the "eaves." Albert Wynyard. Also known as Yorkie, Albert Winter, Peter Wyndham, Bernard De Courcy Wyndham. For the past year he had lived in a different valley, after taking twelve month leases from unsuspecting people and moving out a few months later leaving the rent, phone bills, electricity bills unpaid, property damage, and taking furniture and appliances. He was in debt too at each small local shopping center—grocer, hardware, butcher, garage, as he had taken up residence under the wing, as it were, of the reputation of the owner of each house he rented. Blenheim residents who had been immigrants and had raised their families would arrange the letting of their house before they made their longed-for visit to their home country; or there were those making their dreamed of "overseas tour." There was a middle-aged woman with a cat, another with a garden, who returned to find neither cat nor garden; two couples who returned to find shocking conditions and costs; and others, all trusting the well-dressed young man, who they judged to be not too young to be throwing wild irresponsible parties, not too old to fall ill and be unable to mow the lawn, weed the garden, look after the cat or dog; a bachelor (no women changing the wallpaper, because they didn't like the pattern or the color, or dyeing clothes in the washing machine), and what is more the "right" kind of bachelor—he said he was getting married and was building a house and needed somewhere to stay while he built it; with a handyman's skills, a builder's knowledge; with money to pay the rent (building his own house!). Finally, although Albert Wynyard had both a mustache and a beard, again they were of the "right" kind as worn by TV announcers, anthropologists, and mountaineers, and not by weirdoes and freaks. To the woman with the cat, Wynyard presented himself as a cat lover—he had his own cat, Malcolm, which traveled to work with him in the truck. And when Wynyard noticed paintings in a house, he happened to mention that he was an amateur painter. To the people with lawns and gardens, he described how he talked to the plants and touched them with his green fingers. To those with stereos and pianos he told of his dream of being a composer.

"I'll use your piano, if I may," he said, as if asking a great favor. "I compose, you know."

"You compose?"

How modest he was!

The file gave the facts only, but I, as Alice Thumb, saw the interviews and heard the praises of Albert Wynyard who spoke so sincerely, whose blue eyes shone with honesty in front of the women who, being used to many years of reading romantic novels, perceived this honesty in remembered phrases, "His blue eyes had an honest twinkle . . ."

Yes, he was a real gardener, they said. An outdoor man.

"His skin glowed a healthy tan." (The House By the Lake, Chapter One, Enter Our Hero by Miriam Truly.)

He's worth his weight in gold, they said.

He can turn his hand to anything.

And the Daltons, before they set out on their overseas tour (L.A., Disneyland, Dallas—the spot where Kennedy was assassinated), England (Coronation Street) told their friends, "We feel rather proud to have someone who's a perfect tenant—a handyman, gardener, composer."

Wynyard had also dropped the hint that he was friends with the son of a well-known millionaire, a hint so delicately flavored that it was palatable yet scarcely noticed. It was part of Wynyard's usual serving at each interview and not a highly flavored sauce to enhance the taste of himself as a householder, although this was the result of it, for each houseowner recalled the fact of the millionaire's son and repeated it to relatives and friends and replied to the inevitably sceptical comments with, "Coming from anyone else it could be taken as a way of trying to impress, but Mr. Wynyard isn't like that. Mr. Wynyard is like the answer to a prayer. He's honest. We know people. We can judge."

And when the relatives and friends reminded that it was risky to advertise and accept someone completely unknown, the answer was "We chose Wynyard from a number of applicants." And such was their pride in possessing him that they spoke of their choice as if they confused the granting of tenancy with the adoption of a child.

All who interviewed Albert Wynyard took him at once to their brick and weatherboard, tile roofed and carpeted bosoms.

As a result, in Blenheim alone, several people were now being haunted by Wynyard's debtors and by debt collectors who had only their address in their search for him. It seemed that half of Blenheim was after Wynyard to make him pay, not only as avoider of electricity and telephone bills and rent but as murderer of hopes, of dreams, lawns, citrus trees dead of thirst; and one piano (he must have danced on it, the owners said); and many carpets.

"You read that file as if you were reading a novel," Lance said. "And how's your novel? The one you're writing about your visit to Menton where Margaret Rose Hurndell used to live?" (Margaret Rose Hurndell is our famous writer.)

I didn't pursue that subject. I felt sorry for Lance confronted now by a full scale of good and evil, in Albert Wynyard, removed from a life where a translation which preserved the spirit of the original was "good," the failure of a verb to agree with its subject was bad. Correct answers in

49

examinations were good, incorrect, bad. Enthusiasm was good, apathy bad. Paying attention was good, not paying, bad. This had been his code. My own has similar clarity—a prose sentence which touches like a branding iron is good. A sentence which keeps its feet clean from beginning to end is good. A sentence which, traveling, looks out of portholes as far as horizons and beyond is good. A sentence which goes to sleep is good, if the season is winter; bad, if it is early spring. A sentence which stumbles on useless objects instead of on buried treasure is bad, and worse if it illuminates useless objects with artificial light, but good if it casts a unique radiance upon them.

A word, which is exciting to look at and say and which doesn't slop its meaning over the side, is good; a word which comes up sparkling from the well is good; a word which clusters like last year's bee around last year's flower is bad, if the flower is already dead, but good if the flower is surviving, beautiful, and alone in a place where flowers have not been known to grow and where bees never swarmed before nor gathered nectar.

And so on: such is my code. Perhaps Lance and I married because we both had these elementary codes of good and evil unrelated to the "real" world and its people. Beneath our everyday goods and bads which we erected like a serviceable swing bridge from our somewhere to somewhere else, our day into tomorrow and the next day, there was a mountain river swirling with fashionably recognized goods and evils that had no relation to the French verb or the English prose paragraph; and if we fell from the bridge no clump of vowels or inflated synonyms could help us. I knew it should not have been so; sometimes I felt that I understood Lance's pursuit of the financial "baddies" who were to him like the incorrect answers in an examination, and the person who gave the answers and was therefore a "failure."

"I suppose you'll go after this conman Wynyard?"

"Most certainly."

"Some of your students are enquiring about you. They don't know you've become a debt collector. There's a rumor you've taken up publishing. And another that you've become an agent for The Wonderful World of Science. They'd all be surprised to know what you really do now."

I meant in "real" life which usually means action, the wearing out of muscles and shoe leather, eyesight and skin: that is, undergoing "time," processed by "time."

That evening we sat in our armchairs (six different reclining positions) by the carbonette fire. The tiled fireplace, like the teeth of dinosaurs, gave the age of the house in its cream tiles and the fancy black scroll on each side, these being fashionable decorations and insisted on by the builders when Lewis and I married. Lance and I were living in my house only because his wife had a brother who was a bit funny and needed somewhere to live, and so Lance had given him his old home in Takapuna. There was little trace of my former life in the house, unless it was contained in the structure itself and in one or two details in the rooms which had been redecorated with no children's scuff marks left on the front and back stairs, nor finger marks on the wall near the dining table in the kitchen: my own yesterday was another age.

"The point is," Lance said, "the boss thinks I'll be a success because no one has looked on me as a debt collector. They don't, even now. Those people in Kaka Valley paid up the other day for that dining suite and the glitter-coal electric fire; and the convertible in Churchill Crescent, that uncut moquette mahogany veneer has been settled. Also, the click action in the next street. Deep Sleep, King Size. That's now paid up, without repossession. And I think it may be because I don't look the part of a debt collector. I'm sympathetic."

I was growing used to his new language with its descriptions drawn from advertising of furniture and appliances, with the recurring phrases which, I knew, more than lines of poetry could set the heart of the citizens of Blenheim beating with desire for possession — particularly if the phrases were in fashion, in a language where fashion changes quickly, where once "wall to wall carpet" could inspire as "Glory be to God for dappled things," but no longer; where now "decramastic tiles" satisfies as "pale flakes with fingering stealth."

Our conversation ended, that evening, on the Wynyard file on the usual note with my asking yet again, "But why be a debt collector?"

And I'd stare into the carbonette fire and wonder. Lance Halleton, they used to say, would never "hurt a flea." He was not a "typical" New Zealander. He had never shot and killed and skinned rabbits and strung the skins on the wire fence to dry. I mention this because part of my own childhood was spent watching processes of violence, being horrified by them but not so horrified that I could not marvel, for instance, at the neat fit of skin upon flesh and the consequent neat removal; and the sense of loss and loneliness that what was warm had become cold, in daylight with the sun shining and the fence wire sparkling. I saw animals and birds shot, fish hooked, pets drowned. I had student boyfriends who worked in the freezing works in the holidays, helping to complete the Christmas kill. Lance had never had such a holiday job. He'd never been part of the Killing Season. He's never had to shoot a lame horse or a blind sheepdog or bury a dead cow and her calf. And moving as we do, in a country where sheep and cattle are neighbors, to lame or misbegotten people, when prisoners escaped and took to the bush in the back county, Lance was always appalled by the publicity given to the manhunt which followed and by the hysterical pressure by those who were not prisoners or patients, who were not lame or blind or misbegotten, for the police and their dogs to "get them" and to make more secure those already in custody—in pen or prison. The death of Lance's first wife had been the nearest he came to seeing violence, and even then he saw it remotely, after the crash, when she was made tidy. And he used to say that the war was something which happened elsewhere. (The atom bomb was dropped on his sixteenth birthday.) Even in his practice of sex, in a time before it was freely talked about, he depended on schoolboy metaphor to deny violence and limit his range of feeling, and he never learned to grant his body access to the rich world of his borrowed language, his life work.

Nor had he been one of those men who dream of being other than they are. He had not been a school teacher who longed to be a carpenter or symphony conductor. He had chosen and enjoyed his work. He always took such pleasure in completing a quotation from French or English literature. During our first days of marriage he'd look out at the sun setting with its spectacular ribbons of light and fire over the blue Waitakeres, and recite the whole of the Battle of Blenheim, and although I found the poem irritating and banal I would never have dreamed, then, of saying so. Then, it moved me with deeper love for him. I wonder now how it could have been. It seems impossible and unreal but the reality of the feeling fills the memory to the brim, even though the time is out of reach, and I must believe that together, of an evening, we played out the drama of Old Kaspar at his cottage door, and the unearthed "human skull," the relic of the "famous victory." And that from there we (I) found a likeness in Lance to the same poet's "scholar" which Lance also recited in his old-fashioned elocutionary manner. And from the "thousand bodies rotting in the sun" of Blenheim and the man whose "hopes are with the Dead," he'd turn to the French poetry, keeping strictly to the battles, the shipwrecks, and the cemeteries by the sea.

You can understand how my final question became a set piece for each evening, "But to be a debt collector, and now to hunt a man, Albert Wynyard. Why?"

8.

Our evenings were not all spent at home. Lance went to the Jaguar Club (yes, he was a Jaguar!) while I had my writing class. During the day I spent most of my time in the small study that I'd made out of Edith's bedroom (on the cold side of the house) trying to write my novel while the lessons of the novel-writing course were fresh in my mind. My first two books had been, more or less, "overflow" which everyone has, as when the rain rains down long enough to fill the water tank and you collect the overflow instead of letting it drain away; or you let it drain away and you wait a little longer (perhaps a lifetime) until the soil is fertile enough to grow other than lank lush grass with hollow stalks.

Howard Conway, an American author, had recently set up a school of writing in Central Auckland. He insisted that anyone could write a novel. That seemed fair. "Anyone" was me, I thought, with the advantage of having written two books. Nevertheless, trying to put the teaching into practice seemed more like drudgery—I'd imagined that it would be like watching a fire running along a fuse, against time and life, to explode a once-buried seam of meaning along a disused word-face; and that anything else was "imitation" writing. I still think this is so. I found it hard to write in those days in the small, cold, back room that still had the children's world globe, fingertip control, on the desk—that and the map of the Pacific Ocean floor were the two relics of life with Lewis. I found that all I was writing was family gossip and chat with myself and my past, without a trace of the "art."

What did Howard Conway know about it, anyway? I asked myself. He was young, charming, and he'd written two novels, *Seed on the Shore*, and *Leaf in the Wind*, both in a kind of blowaway tradition — women with streaming hair and eyes, horses with flowing manes, and trees and men with flowing seed, set in storm and hurricane country. These novels combined with Howard Conway's appearance, and his constant urging, pour it all out, gave him an anchorless air, and one could not imagine him pausing long enough by a ream of typing paper to tether a novel.

Writing was in fashion at the time, I remember, and that partly explained the success of the writing school. There'd been the famous poet's death, and he was often talked of in Blenheim, and some said that he was wearing his skin with the inside out and it must have hurt even to have the air touch it, and that he'd been born that way, with his skin put on the way we taught our children to put on their socks — outside in, then quick-flip, and the warm side is in and the ridged side out, and there's no hurting, but with the poet something went wrong in the putting on, a ridged side was there for life, inside and hurting.

The other more recent death (he had died since I returned from my travels) was that of Peter Wallstead, a little-known novelist who suddenly became known and greatly admired when his books, long out of print, were re-issued (after his death), and the critics spent most of their space saying how extraordinary Peter Wallstead had been, a history teacher living and teaching all those years in a small town and apparently never wanting to leave the *Maniototo*. His work became less analyzed than the fact of his having stayed in the *Maniototo*, surely the last place a writer would want to be! What was the Maniototo? people asked. Where was it? Not everyone in the north knows the geography of the south, and even some in the south did not know. It was a high plain, they were told, in Central Otago—you know, where the air is known to be rare, where apricots grow, and there's a scheme to drown the land and the towns. Central Otago with its battle-place names — Naseby, Glencoe, Cromwell — and the Maniototo itself where Peter Wallstead lived, didn't it mean a plain of blood after the battles fought there? But wasn't it also a place where patients went to be cured of their sicknesses?

There was some concern that Peter Wallstead had been missed from the literary scene. The deprivation was terrible. Fancy his staying all those years in the Maniototo and never even going to Wellington! He'd been a P.E.N. member, too. Why hadn't anyone known about him? Just P. Wallstead . . . Why hadn't anyone seemed to know how good he was? Why hadn't he come to live in Auckland, the cosmopolitan city, to get experience, to keep his art alive and in the swim? What swim was there in the Maniototo where everything froze in winter?

Dead, Peter Wallstead was swirled into the swim as if the Clutha had burst its banks. He was gone, missed, and they published photos of him with his chin on his hand and a sly see-you've-missed-me smile on his lips and in his eyes. He had a large smooth face like a country. He must have known about all the battles of history; and goodness knew what he had discovered on that secret plain. Just imagine if he had visited Auckland or Blenheim! Or had he, in secret? Who knew? And although few people coming north had lived in the Maniototo, it became fashionable to say, making it sound mysterious and desirable, as "overseas" used to be, before people discovered that mystery and imagination are for everyone (and didn't Peter Wallstead prove it?).

"When I was living in the Maniototo . . ."

There were some who believed the place didn't exist, there was so much mystery about it, and mention of it could strike a roomful of people silent, thinking their own thoughts, wondering, fearing, imagining.

"When I was living in the Maniototo . . ."

Already you see, although Blenheim had more crime and suicide than other cities, it also had more history. The man who "discovered" Peter Wallstead lived on the outskirts of Blenheim, and he too was touched by the everlasting ripple of fame and by the name, Maniototo.

When Lance came home from work he sometimes said that his customers had mentioned Wallstead or the dead poet, for Blenheim owned them both now. Lance was learning to know Blenheim — the houses and gardens — the strange assortment of houses, some, like ours, dated by the peppermint stripes, green and white, on the weatherboards by the front porch, others with stone archways and heavy carved doors labeled Mediterranean; those with new false bricks and real bricks over false bricks, and false iron and false wood, and various house-skins or "cladding"; swimming pools in different shapes and depths; pebble gardens; riverstones at the front door; streams, fountains, wishing wells where gnomes sat or stood idle or fished — many gnomes, for these were made in Blenheim, in Kaka Valley, where the factory yard was stacked with finished and unfinished gnomes; houses with Swiss letterboxes, English letterboxes, no fences, plastic and wooden fences, with and without gates, lowline, highline; trees that burst in summer with delicate blue blossoms (lasseandra) or strong fierce red blossoms (rata) or with clouds of pink, cream-silk, apricot (these the oleanders) or quick-growing trees that snapped easily, and bled; coast trees, salt and wind-loving shrubs, native plants—flax, pittosporum, pink and white manuka, kaka beak, pohutukawa — while inside the houses there were the carpets named Sky Planet, Dream of the Night, Forest Splendor, Classic Plains, Mountain Glory, upon which rested the pseudo-mahogany wall-units, color TV sets, furniture with cabriole legs, turned legs, ranch-slider doors lounge suites, rocking chairs or fixed chairs with or without arms with or without footstool, convertible, nonconvertible . . .

You see, that time in Blenheim's life, indeed in the

country's life, was the time where the blossoming and naming of furniture and objects for the home replaced the breeding and naming of race horses in importance; when passion was less between husband and wife than between person and furnishing — different models, textures, uses. Sex became a matter of interior gloss and washable surfaces. I know that a woman like myself, at home all day, could spend every hour dreaming of the house and its furnishings, while a man like Lance could fill his mind entirely with nails, hammers, motor mowers, sanders, concrete mixers. It was a time of rich material culture as vivid and exciting as that of a land where, say, there is a flourishing of literature or great music; except that this renaissance was lacking a soul, the satisfaction was a gloss, a chemical protection with no relation to human weather, and yet, because poetry is attendance upon the world, still with every relation to the dead poet and the fluttering piwakwaka or black fantail.

And yet—how could people compete for love with their undercoat and their uncut moquette? A woman spied on by her wall-unit would grow anxious; smooth wall paint sneered at wrinkled human skin.

"And I tell you," Lance said, "only in the older homes is any of that stuff paid for."

He grew more vindictive, more earnest about the debts and the debtors and the urgency of tracking down Albert Wynyard.

"I'll make them pay," he said. "And when I do catch up with Yorkie Wynyard."

He preferred to call him "Yorkie" thus reminding him and me that Wynyard was not a "real" New Zealander, and so what more could one expect from a "foreigner"?

"I can't believe you mean that," I said. "You're not the type to put pressure on people for money. They're young families. Life's hard enough."

"They must pay."

I could see why Rob Guthrie was impressed.

"You'll be hated," I said. "I don't see how we can keep on living in Blenheim after this. I'm ashamed of the kind of work you're doing now. From the humanities, from language which never harmed anyone, to this!"

Lance stared at me.

"You, of all people! Language that never harmed anyone. Ha, Ha. I've known more rape and murder and debt in language than there'll ever be in Blenheim. Suicide too! This is what partly persuaded me to give up teaching language."

So that was it. Another reason. His new attitude could be blamed on words and on his being a part of the Great New Zealand Dream of Punish, Punish, which meant you had to have someone to punish, a "them" and so you were forever dividing and destroying. I had been more comfortable believing Lance's new work was mostly the result of his age, a desire for drastic change to try to outwit the imposition of time. After all, everyone was quite happy to say that my own interest in writing was related to my age.

"At least a novel doesn't prosecute or haunt anyone."

"I wouldn't be too sure. And we both know, don't we, that the debt collector as well as the debtor can be haunted.

"Of course."

He looked so tired and pale and burdened. There was nothing he could do about his obsession, and my complaints only increased his suffering which itself was unreal, a veneer of suffering, a replica which we both had to treat as the "real thing" thus cheapening or even making counterfeit our exchange of love.

Six months later, Lance was dead. Perhaps those who knew him will say that he confused the pursuit of a notorious debtor with the pursuit of living and when one had been found the other was no longer desired. Let me explain.

9.

It was one of those days when winter starts trying out its range of weather to see which can give the most discomfort and misery while ensuring that a complaint from one person to another brings the reply, "It could be much worse; it's not snowing, like down south; or frosty; and it's not even raining all the time," and a feeling of shame at being unable to cope with weather that is declared "ordinary." It was a sly, public day and being in it was like being in a leaking bus shelter waiting for a bus that was late or never came; it was a day of everlasting afternoon.

Lance worked all day, still wearing the ridiculous uniform of the debt collector—he'd bought himself a panama hat, a striped maroon and white blazer, a discard from the old boys of one of the secondary schools in Auckland, gym shoes, and the kind of "walk" shorts, grey, to the knee, which doctors and bank officers wear in Auckland in the summer. He'd even bought a fishing fly for his hat.

We were both going out that evening — Lance to his Jaguars (they were decorating the new sports pavillion up near Heavenfield Mall), and I to my writing class, and as I would not be home when Lance finished work I left some ham sandwiches and a salad for tea, food fitting to the dreariness of the day, evoking memories of rained on picnics, irritations, sunburn, and the kind of useless crying that in children is called "grizzling." No doubt, opposing the mood of the weather, I might have made soup or stew, but I was in a compliant mood—if the day says weep then why not weep?

That evening our class discussed writing in the first person, or what I used to call the "I-book." When I was a child, I'd open a book and if I found it was written in the first person I'd say with disgust, "Oh, an 'I' book," and quickly shut it and refuse to read it. I think I could not bear the imposition of the invisible "I," nor, in order to make it come alive, did I feel that I could surrender my everyday self and life to become the "I." Brought up on western films and on the love lyrics of the time, "Darling, I surrender," I found the power of the "I" writer over the reader too confusing and eroding. Later, I learned not to refuse the demands of an "I-book," although I was invariably uneasy, especially since I began writing, at the separation between the "I" and the characters of the story, and the enormous burden upon the "I" to "tell all" while viewing through the narrow I-shaped window that restricted the vision and allowed only occasional arrows to be fired with no guarantee that they would pierce the armor of "otherness" worn by the characters of the book. The success of an I-book seemed to rely on the perfection of the arrows and of the aim, and nothing less than perfection would pass the test, and it was no use avoiding that truth by trying to make the writer into a god or goddess with perfect vision. A writer taking on the "I," takes a straight line that can be turned upon itself to become a circle or curved to become a hook or left alone as a prelude to infinity or have its back broken into the hypotenuse, the opposite, the adjacent.

I listened resentfully while Howard Conway gave us his own rules about the first person.

"Never use it," he said, and I might have been surprised by his tidy air of caution had I not realized that a skin-trapped "I" could have no place in the writing of such a roving omniscient as Conway. I might have been more tolerant of him that evening had the ordinary Auckland rain not been so extraordinarily thorough in its dispensing of wet and misery and a feeling of homelessness. I was eager to get home and rejoice that our basement was never flooded, our roof didn't leak, the water didn't find slits in the flashing to seep through the top of the windows.

Also, we owed money to no one.

To hell with Howard Conway, I thought. He was wearing two-tone shoes, which increased the diluting of his image into Cloud-Carried Novelist Pale Wash. He was wearing a uniform, too — a striped suit of seersucker that American tourists wear abroad and American tennis spectators and poets wear at home.

I left the writing class without waiting for our usual coffee and literary chat. I arrived home to find that Lance had gone to bed. I took the tray of ham sandwiches and went to the bedroom

"You didn't go to Jaguars," I said, accusingly. "Let's have a picnic."

He was only half awake but he sat up, looking rather pale and confused.

"Ham sandwiches," I said. "Who cares about the first person? Is anything wrong?"

He frowned. "I can't believe it," he said. "I caught up with Yorkie Wynyard. I've got him at last."

"Do you really want to eat ham sandwiches?" he asked, pushing the plate away.

"Yorkie Wynyard! Well . . . they're a picnic, and rain, and traveling and mosquitoes and the beach. Lewis and I took the children up north once or twice. We ate ham sandwiches and pine needles and we always came home feeling ragged. Tell me about Yorkie Wynyard."

We snuggled up.

"Tell me," I said. His body felt different. He'd been using all parts of himself as weapon, hook, springing trap, rope,

62

cage, pitfall, decoy to catch the chief debtor, and now that he had found him, he felt warm as if he'd spent all day and evening in a bath; he had returned to warm first person country, away from the struggle of tenses, the perfect, pluperfect, present historic. How can I explain? He had become existential. He "nullified the possibility of death."

"It was like a dream," he said. "Perhaps it didn't happen. It was in the next valley, near that grove of trees before the bus turns to go to the top of the hill."

"The pine trees?"

"Yes. But they're a special sort, light green. By that spillover discount shop. He was standing looking at the row of disinfectants. They were selling them off cheap, they were all a brick color and labeled Carnation. They looked like urine. He was dressed exactly as I was — even to the fishing fly in his panama hat, and at first I thought it was someone from the Takapuna territory, not working, just browsing, and then he turned and I recognized him at once. Yorkie Wynyard. Masquerading as a debt collector. He didn't even try to deny it, he just laughed, a hearty laugh, in the open air; you could see how he conned everyone. He'd collected hundreds of dollars from the valley, just this morning. Everyone paid up. He boasted about it, a real skite."

"Did you get the police or anything?"

"I suppose I could have made a citizen's arrest. I rang the police, and Rob Guthrie. We just wait and see. But I caught him, and we know what he's up to."

I was surprised that Lance was no longer vindictive. I almost began to hope that, now he had found Yorkie Wynyard, he would return to teaching.

"It's a long way," I said, "from la lune blanche luit dans les bois."

He smiled gently. "I might have dreamed it," he said.

He got out of bed and went across to the dressing table and looked in the mirror. He traced with his hand the outline of his forehead and cheek and chin, and as he moved his arm forward, he tipped over the plate of ham sandwiches and they came unstuck and the ham fell out. Tongue-pink. I'd made them from a thick 'n' thin loaf, the thick end as the thin had already been used.

"It was a mistake," I said. "I shouldn't have made ham sandwiches."

Lance returned to bed and we switched off the light.

"It's not the weather for ham sandwiches," I said with a strange determination to be mundane. "Why were you looking in the mirror?"

"Something I thought of," he said.

We snuggled again. I could tell that he was smiling in the dark, a smile without hooks or traps.

"De chaque branche part une voix . . ."

He completed the quotation, as he used to do, triumphantly as if to say, Ah, what a memory!

Two hours later, in his sleep, he coughed violently, and died. They said it was an inexplicable spasm in his throat that choked him. I was almost too angry to mourn. Fiction would have arranged it better, I thought. And yet it would be thrown out of fiction as unforgiveable. The pronouns, tenses, participles, past and present, would fight to exclude it. And for all I know he might have choked on a remembered idiom.

10.

My son Noel was very helpful when Lance died. He played the role of the Blue Fury in smoothing and erasing. I met once again old Lewis Barwell's wife, the drain-laying millionairess, and the newest Barwell replica—a baby son for Noel and Sonia. They already had a daughter, Binnorie, aged six, with a glandular complaint that resulted in giantism. Noel may have supposed that his knowledge of a wide range of diseases gave him the privilege of being able to choose from them; and the unacceptable fact that he'd not been able to choose had made both him and Sonia into If-Only parents.

"If only it had been measles or polio or anything else. Little Binny."

I was swirled temporarily back into the current of my former life, and because I did not want to get caught in it (by a weed or by a dead branch from a distant tree) or held under and drowned by a stone, I made plans to leave Blenheim.

Noel still has his office in Heavenfield Mall, next to the aviary of golden birds singing in the artificial light. He is at the heart of Heavenfield Mall, although I know that he once had a longing to practice in the country, perhaps in a forestry town where the children go barefoot from choice and ride bareback on the wild black horses. It helps me to know that he has this dream, that he and Sonia do not rely solely on the dream which still persuades them to buy tiny tables and chairs, children's furniture, for a child who could never fit into them.

I sold the Bannockburn home and bought a house in Stratford where I live now and where I'm writing this version of my story.

11.

I confess that I rejoiced in being alone once again, for I had exercised and developed a faculty of aloneness during my long stay in the hospital, and in spite of my now being able to say, in bus queues and waiting rooms and on railway platforms, "Do you know, I have buried two husbands?", the habit of corporate living had been more spectacular and wayward than refined and strengthened, and I easily became a single person again, while cherishing that prime remark which gives interest and meaning to bus and rail queues.

I missed the pleasures of sex and the accompanying habit of directing and receiving love, of someone being present in all seasons, of singing each to each like birds, and replying (although Lewis and I, as I have said, had "utility" conversations, Pass me, Fetch me, Did you see, Have you read, etc., while Lance and I had "commentary" conversations as if we two were reporting events to a third party), but I enjoyed the tidy selfishness of being alone, without explanation or promise, expectation of disappointment. I came to believe that I had buried two husbands only because I had been caught in the general pattern of the world about me which is hard to break without an act of violence or unreason, and if one does want to change it, one must be forever in a state of watchfulness; and so, after Lance died, when I finally cleaned my heart out like a good heartwife, I set to work at last, seriously, on my writing while I planned another visit, possibly to Edith in London, certainly to the United States to stay in Baltimore with Brian Wilford, to New York perhaps, and to California to stay with the poet I met during my first visit. With the little writing I'd done in Blenheim before Lance died I might just as well not have gone to Howard Conway's writing school, for all I appeared to have learned was a list of forbidden acts put forever out of reach like certain augmented intervals of harmony which nevertheless abound in the works of the "real" composers. I decided to break the rules, not because I felt my writing would even approach the shadow of perfection, but because nothing in art is forbidden. By critics and teachers, yes. By the painters, writers, composers, sculptors, no. It is daunting enough for a writer to face the natural forbiddings of her imperfections and weaknesses which are more convincing in their Thou Shalt Nots than all the commandments of those who try to teach the art of writing. I have never been able to accept that writing a novel or poem is like shopping or gardening—you decide to do it and you do it, and that's that—at least not unless you decide to rob a bank in the shopping area or plant your garden under the sea or in the sky, and even then you do not decide but have your actions decided for you. And then you shop only because you are starving and you garden because you must plant food for your mouth or your heart and mind.

Shall I put it another way, with verse from the *Manifold*?

I am not Scalene, old warrior with the shortened foot
                                                    hobbling by,
nor isosceles prayer-pointing the sky,
but part of the whole only, hypotenuse,
my life stared at, paid away
by the rightness of an angle's right eye.

*

When I, Scarlet Tanager, returned from that wonderful
                    summer in the south

68

to find pond and lake icily indifferent to my thirst,
mounds of snow waiting to complete my burial,
every shiftless wood unprepared to provide a green meal,
I had no strength or time to tell about it in the usual way;
while my wings in rhythmic memory still answered the
                                    winds' buffeting
and I shook the sea-salt from my feathers and the sun and
            the stars out of my eyes,
too tired, I clung then to the lowest bough making my only
            possible statement
—scarlet on white,
an image long interpreted
as bloody fact or threat.

As the snow's diminishing became certain, I learned again
            to survive,
I found food served by the repentant blossoming wood.
And then, my blood-color furled, I flew to the highest.
            bough and I sang
in detail, without violence, a civilized version of my story.

                              *

12.

I am Hypotenuse.
Here burdened by the weight of opposite and adjacent
proved equal to others, never to myself,
I square with myself for the satisfaction of others who count
more than I
who lie as thin as a garden line in my fleshless body
who lie and square and cube and carry and join.
I am Hypotenuse. I close in
a shape that is nameless without my prison.
Larger than opposite and adjacent I yet suffer their corner
— creating presence,
the shadows formed in the crook of our shepherded lives;
the corner of the paddock where the fence is propped up,
strained,
the grass grows through the bright barbed wire; mushrooms
appear
overnight; the old horse stands to drop his hot cone of
straw-filled manure.

I am Hypotenuse of a southern country. I fence, perhaps, a
farm overlooking the Tasman.
Pages turn, touch my boundaries, black print, underlinings
underlined.
And some day I will write my still-riddling memoirs
beginning,
"Pythagoras and I . . . ."

Should time diminish me I shall become the sine, the
                opposite, the cosine, the adjacent, when,
ignoring what I have been we two will play tangent aerially
among the stars shapen and mis-shapen.
Someone said to me,
"There's quite a lot to write about, considering.
I've thought out lots of stories in my spare time
— you know — plots, characters, all kinds of drama,
and some day I might have a go at writing.
Plenty do
and get away with it,
and make a fortune.
It's knowing what the readers want
and having an eye on television and film rights,
something they can turn into a script
quick as a wink, like that, nothing fancy only
good old-fashioned drama
that gets you locked to the page or screen
— you know what I mean. I tell you,
I might try it.
There's a great deal to write about
that hasn't been thought of before
and I might just give it a go."

He had a steam-cleaning business
and got rid of ants, borer, fleas as extra.
He could clean your house-walls on the outside
and kill everything inside, except pets and people. Rats and
                mice were extra.
"How do you do it," I asked.
"It dries up their secretions. They become shells," he said.
"See. It says on the packet.
as for the steam-blasting, you just hose, under pressure."
"Why don't you try writing your novel?" I said.
So he wrote his novel. You might think I'm going to say
He's a mere shell now
no longer a pest,

that under pressure his old skin is peeling away.
but I'm not going to say that, although I'm tempted.
He did try. He tried sincerely,
but his *want* burned away in the exercise, his *want*
became a shell.
No, he didn't give up.
He didn't say, "I'll stick to steam-cleaning and borer-
    bombs."
He unloaded all his stored-up drama
which fell apart at birth, lacking the life-dealing want.
No one told him that his want should fill the world,
that to write you have to be at the terrible point of loss,
and stay there, wanting to write, wanting in, not out.
Certainly, it's a rat and mouse life,
a life-burned sun
and no sweet pesticide
and no cleaning, weatherproofing,
no possible preserving from exposure;
and even words, as paintwork, won't hold under pressure.

There are so many people going the other way.
There are those who, trained to write poems,
carry a kit of tales about the prince, the princess, the beast,
and the green, ripe, poisoned fruit;
and as they pass, to keep their screaming hand supple,
they chainsaw the avenue of trees, they mow every lawn in
    sight;
knocking at the stranger's door, they ask
Please may we cut and plane the wood, hammer the nails in.

A thousand birds pass overhead.
The center pages of the newspaper are devoted to spring
                    and summer fashions.
Other pages carry rugby and racing news, and the story of
    the man
who earns his claim to 5,000 acres of land
through his command of a world market in semen.

And still the concert singers Come up from Somerset,
or Roll Down regularly to Rio.
The people, so many of them, rush by,
not being able to fly.

And I open the bud of one more birthday
finding it as usual not perfect,
got at by something before I can protect what
I imagine might be its permitted integrity.

An ally of simplicity
I woke early.

The hungry cat goes out in the grey morning.

Sentences are the smallest bedrooms.
Sit, sleep, love.
Eat and write at the table.

O how all those absent are brought by force to mind,
dissected, picked over
for a stray share to put
on the table's empty page and plate.

The fed cat
sleeps on the mat.

PART TWO

Paying Attention to The Ice Pick, The Diamond Account Book, A Family Heirloom and an Invitation.

13.

For a brief period after Lance's death, when I had settled in my Stratford home (an old three-bedroom house on Miranda Street, opposite the hospital), and was trying to organize my novel and get used to a town full of sky, English flowers, bloody history and the taste of snow, I found myself (as the saying is) "going to seed." Perhaps "she's going to seed" is the second most treasured sentence in the phrase book of the bus stop and the railway waiting room. I find that I have a verse about it, from the Manifold.

Yes, I am going to seed. I know it.
After being eaten for so many years,
cut, recut, forced to branch this way and that,
I have grown tall, I have put forth small white flowers,
I look over fences into people's faces.
Bees glance at me, the wind has taken me in hand.
My taste is too strong and sour, my growth is rank.
People frown to see me put down yet one more root.

The invitation from Brian Wilford to return to Baltimore and write my novel there, came three years ago at the end of a motor-mowing, chain-sawing Stratford summer spent beneath an echoing corrugated iron sky that was softened only by the frothing azaleas and the rain-scarf of every few days. I was pleased to accept Brian's invitation. My memories of Baltimore presented themselves, as memories do, changed in shape with new clothes and colors for the occasion, but I quickly identified their substance — the snow, the "weather," the dead poets of Blenheim and Baltimore; Tommy and the Blue Fury; objects, like the ice pick; people, like Mrs. Tyndall.

With my rank growth and my proliferation of roots and a travel handbag of memories I returned to Baltimore toward the end of the northern winter. I had deceived myself into thinking that one or two deaths of relatives and friends may give immunity, at least for a few years, but even that year there was no immunity, and I see now how close death is to the process of "going to seed," for both are merely an abundance of life which shocks and frightens by its untidiness, its lack of boundaries and the finality of its choice of a place to grow.

Strangely enough, the ice pick and Mrs. Tyndall come to mind now together, both as part of Brian's life and my work and the kind of pain that makes a writer want to throw away the words that are screens, moveable walls, decorations, unnecessary furniture, and keep only the load-bearing words (the load-bearing birds?) that stop the sky from falling.

First, the ice pick. It was kept at the top of the stairs near the barred window looking out over the alley. "It's my only weapon," Brian said.

I suspected he would never use it. He kept it as he kept the stained canvas rucksack of his young days, varnished and preserved within a frame on the wall, as a reminder of time spent in the southern Alps of New Zealand and of his first view of the Matukituki Valley. I have never seen the valley. It embodied Brian's dream of serenity and wild beauty, and it was partly his fear of losing the dream which made him keep the rusted ice pick with the broken handle. If he chose to keep a special memory, he embalmed an object rather than an image. His house was crowded with objects, many of them works of art, and others, like the ice pick and the rucksack and the hammer and plane that had belonged to his father, preserved as personal works of art,

78

kinds of memories more reliable than the usual fading image, a retouched part of his life, guaranteed not to fade, yet also, like the ice pick, useful as a means of destruction in the cause of self-preservation. And at the time of my visit to Brian's house there was much talk of self-preservation, not in the sense of embalming, varnishing, but in surviving attack, for the city had one murder every day and many more robberies and muggings with violence both random and familial, and it was useless for a visitor to cry out, "It's not my fault, I wasn't here in the beginning, I have no part in your city and your country's history, look at me, see how kind I am, how I smile, it's not my fault, see, I am different, I am a stranger." Such pleas were self-evident lies, particularly in a city where the known poet died, and the responsibility of the truth brought gloom and hopelessness: I was not a stranger, I was there in the beginning, with the others.

In the general demand for weapons and seeing an advertisement in the local newspaper, and with example of the ice pick in mind, I bought from the bargain store down Monument Street, a tear gas *pen* in a small thin box, like the box for a fountain pen, the kind that used to be popular for presents at Christmas and on birthdays. I called myself a writer and this special pen had been advertised as one with special cartridges that could disable an attacker, perhaps cause momentary blindness, yet, because it was still "only a pen" (it said so on the label, didn't it?) I bought it, and when I unwrapped it I was horrified to read the first sentence in the leaflet enclosed, Instructions for using your tear gas *gun*.

A simple mix-up of language. I ought to have known. The ice pick for use as blood-pick and past-pick. I can still hear my cry, "But it's supposed to be a pen!"

I never used it. I put it away, guiltily, and when Mrs. Tyndall, who came twice a week to clean the house, found it she knew at once what it was, she was horrified, knowing that pens are no longer refilled with ink, only with gas and explosives. I could say "as usual" but I will tell you about Mrs. Tyndall.

14.

Mrs. Tyndall lived with her daughter and her family across town. Her routine seldom varied. As Brian left for work at half past eight in the morning, Mrs. Tyndall arrived with her two large shopping bags—one empty, for carrying home the food that Brian gave her, the other holding her personal things for the day—a sweater, a magazine or two, an overall, perhaps photos of her daughter and her daughter's children. She'd go down the basement stairs, carefully, for they had no handrail, to the cupboard where the cleaners and dusters were kept, and while she was there I'd perform my routine of switching down the thermostat to what I thought was a reasonable sixty-five. Then, five or ten minutes later, Mrs. Tyndall reappeared, ready for work, with cleaning materials and Brian's old radio in one basket, and the vacuum cleaner under her arm, and as soon as she had struggled, refusing my help, to the top of the stairs, she would put everything down on the floor, say, Whew, Whew, and reach out and turn up the thermostat to her comfortable eighty-five. Then she'd plug in the radio and switch it to the station that each morning gave out a magic number which had to be remembered, for the radio station phoned at random during the day and if by chance it was your phone and you said, quickly, the magic number, then you won the jackpot, hundreds of dollars, or a color TV, washing machine, stereo, or a holiday for two in Florida. At the end of winter when the weather was having a last savage fling, there were many people who dreamed of going to Florida, not because they wanted to or they knew what they would find there, but because it was part of the general dream. Every time the phone rang Mrs. Tyndall rushed to answer it and give the magic number. She never gave up hope. "This might be it," she'd say. She believed that although the station said it phoned at random it would be more likely to choose a doctor's house. She never expected the phone to ring at her daughter's place, a long bus ride across town to a poor district just off the beltway, that had no famous hospital to give it distinction, just miles and miles of row houses of decaying crumbling brick, with smashed in windows and tide-marks of litter out in the street, beachcombed by the children and the occasional bands of young adults, the workless and the hopeless, and by the stray dogs that prowled in packs in Druid Hill Park, which separated downtown from the suburbs and was crowned by a zoo, where the people went in fear, not of the caged animals, but of the murderers and muggers.

When I told Mrs. Tyndall I sometimes took a bus from outside Brian's house to Druid Hill Park she was shocked. "Never go walking there." But it was the name that fascinated me. Druid Hill Park. Was it here that the wolves howled on the night of my first visit to Baltimore? I know there had been a pack of wild dogs that set upon and devoured two children. And once I saw a chimpanzee, dressed in human clothing and carrying a handbag, out walking along in the park. I did not dream it. The chimpanzee lived in a house near by, with a man and woman. It slept in a bed and ate at a table with knife and fork. One day it was missing and they found it on Howard Street North dressed as I had seen it, but among a crowd of shoppers in the five and dime store.

As Mrs. Tyndall went about her work and I moved from room to room to let her work freely, I tried to imagine her feelings about Brian's home. Her own home was perhaps just as comfortable, for her daughter had a good job at the hospital. It was clear that she looked with some contempt on Brian's collection of objects, especially as it was one of her duties to dust them, but it was when she opened the refrigerator door and gazed at the shelves packed with food, suddenly lit up like a secret altar, that her dark eyes glittered and I saw in them an unashamed desire to pack all the food in her shopping bags and leaving the rest of the house "undone" (she did the "upstairs" after lunch) go home and never return. The fact that downstairs in the boiler room beside the basement room where I worked during the day but did not yet sleep at night, for the weather was still cold, Brian kept an older refrigerator packed with "extra" food, impressed Mrs. Tyndall, I could see, to the point of making her feel dizzy and confused. In her life and the life of her relations and friends, food was eaten; there was never enough to keep; the only things she kept, apart from those for use, were photographs glossy and colored, of the family, and her bottle of gall stones.

"There's an old refrigerator in the basement, there's nothing much in it," Brian had explained to Mrs. Tyndall. But I had seen her face when she opened the door on the suddenly illuminated TV dinners, cheese cakes, canned beer, apple sauce.

Because she was of an older generation, she had learned to suppress or dismiss the desire for a fair share of the world's goodies. Had she been younger she might have behaved like one of those who stormed down Fifth Avenue one evening, raiding the most exclusive shops for the "white man's sweaters." Or she might have been like my friend Beatrice who took her inspiration for struggle from Chopin and the courage of discipline from Bach, and tried to "rise above," as the saying goes (as if those who tried to do so were equipped as automatic angels), the slums of Philadelphia where her childhood gifts had persuaded a teacher to give her piano lessons at a reduced rate, something for which neither her fellow pupils at school nor the privileged children the other side of the railway tracks ever forgave her. But hers is another story.

At lunch time I'd buy two hotdogs and Mrs. Tyndall and I would sit in the tiny kitchen drinking our tea and trying to decide the right amount of leverage to move the hotdog from plate to mouth without spraying ourselves and each other with stripes of onion and blobs of sauce. Every now and again Mrs. Tyndall would say, "Thank you for the hotdogs, it was very kind of you," in a false sounding voice, and I'd feel depressed that such gulfs have been made between people, and people with the one forced into gratitude for nothing, the other self-appointed in the role of benefactor.

"Dr. Brian is very good to me," she'd say as she was leaving, pointing to her bag of food. Yet, there was a glitter of contempt in her dark eyes. We both knew she was too old and too tired to be slaving for Master Clean, Bright and White.

"You'll listen to the radio for the numbers?" she'd say as I let her out into the grey street.

I'd promise.

Then seeing the falling snow I'd say, "You can't go out in this weather," realizing that I was speaking with the same falseness as she spoke her gratitude, yet we both had meant what we said. I knew she would go as she was used to being in all weathers, and she'd stand on the corner by the supermarket, without shelter, waiting for the infrequent number five bus.

She'd even refuse to take Brian's umbrella.

"Oh no, he'll need it."

I saw her small dark face smile and her brown eyes glitter with delight in escaping once again from Dr. Brian and his over-furnitured house and his all-white bathroom with its foaming bleach and other poisonous-fumed cleaners filling the house like incense; and the heavy vacuum cleaner to be dragged up and down the stairs; and the wave of sickness and dizziness that overcame her as she stooped to brush the carpet at each stair tread. She smiled in real bliss. She was her own person again.

I'd then close and lock the front door. Then I'd go at once to the thermostat and switch it from the stifling eighty-five to my comfortable sixty-five. I too was my own person again.

During that winter month Mrs. Tyndall and I became formal friends with our two meeting-points the magic numbers over the radio, and the hope for the jackpot, and God's Diamond Account Book and the hope for a miracle.

The Diamond Account book and an explanatory leaflet came in the mail the same week that the posters appeared in front of the old movie house on Monument Street, next to the wig shop and the strip-tease club.

"Four Miracles a Day. Ten a.m. 2 p.m. 5 p.m. 8 p.m. Hear Brother Coleman. Open God's Diamond Account Book."

Mrs. Tyndall, who had already received her book, as they'd been delivered first across town, explained how for five dollars a month, sent to Brother Coleman's Mission in California, God would fulfill all needs, particularly the need for cars, washing machines, new furniture, houses. Brother Coleman had this financial arrangement with God, a partnership that you, too, could buy, if you kept up your payments. Both the leaflet and the book had testimonials showing photographs of delighted people standing at their front door receiving their washing machine or automobile; others, enraptured, pointing towards their new home or their new wheelchair (God having paid for the operation which enabled them to leave their bed).

The leaflet explained that there were those who had paid their five dollars regularly each month until one day a stranger came to their door saying, "May I speak to the occupant or householder?" "Good morning, Sir or Madam

84

you have won a brand new home with drapes, carpets, all furnishings and furniture in the place of your choice, the taxes paid twenty years in advance." There were others who had been ill and couldn't pay the doctor or the hospital and yet they'd managed the five dollars a month, even from their social welfare checks, and suddenly one day they found themselves cured, or they received a phone call, long distance, to say they'd been left five or ten thousand dollars. The photograph in the leaflet showed someone waving the check in the air, with an inset of Brother Coleman smiling and saying, "They paid into God's Diamond Book" and holding a small bank, like a bankbook, with a row of sparkling stuff, like diamonds, on the cover.

"They look like real diamonds," I said, when Mrs. Tyndall showed me her Diamond Account Book. On the first page there was a sample check such as might be received, with the words, "God from the Diamond Bank in Heaven authorizes you to receive whatever you wish," followed by a scrawled signature, as checks must be signed. The signature read G-O-D.

"Of course the diamonds aren't real," Mrs. Tyndall said hastily, "but they do sparkle."

I agreed to her request to go to hear Brother Coleman at the Roxy and to report back to her, when she came to work in three days' time, about the miracles he had performed. She couldn't go herself, she said, because she was too busy and it was too far away to cross town at night, and when I suggested that she could go from Brian's place, perhaps to the ten o'clock miracle, she said, no, she wanted to be told about it.

"Everyone's talking about him," she said.

A feeling of misery came over me: I knew there were secret fears, problems she didn't talk about, situations that Brian and I and others took for granted, that for her were full of alarm and threat. I'd seen the same confusion in the face of a deaf person or of an old man who couldn't read, trying to decipher the traffic signal "walk" or "wait," so he could cross the road safely.

I remember she took special care that day in cleaning the bathroom, the hardest room in the house to clean, with the bath and the shower, the lavatory and the basin and floor to be scoured, disinfected, polished. I sensed that she most disliked the bathroom and that at her age — she was in her late sixties — she found the stooping and kneeling and leaning distressing and tiring. I knew, too, from my New York friend Beatrice that the bathroom was looked on as the white person's domain, for they, with black skin, had always been encouraged to think that their skin was unclean (I had seen the bottles of skin bleach still displayed in the drug stores); and by the time Mrs. Tyndall had cleaned the bathroom and knelt at the tile-surrounded bath and the furred lavatory altar she at last came to life with a kind of whirling rage at the indignity her race had suffered, and in accordance with the role of the Blue Fury within the bottle of cleanser she erased all trace of Brian and me from the bathroom.

Once again I said goodbye to her at the door, and I promised to go the next day to witness Brother Coleman's miracle.

15.

The next day I set out to witness Brother Coleman's ten o'clock miracle, as I supposed that his first advertised miracle of the day would be more fresh, untouched by the assaults of afternoon and evening when blood was running down the sky and the Baltimore day ended in a turmoil of fumes and noise and death.

The snow was melting into slush, rain, and sleet. I wore my secondhand fur coat from the Veterans. When I arrived at the Roxy I recognized Brother Coleman at once from his photo. He stood at the door with two large assistants who looked like henchmen or bouncers out of a gangster movie, greeting the crowd drawn from all over the city in response to their needs and his advertising—people on crutches, in wheelchairs, with hunched backs, deformed bodies, withered arms, wearing the dark glasses and carrying the white sticks of the blind. The old Roxy filled rapidly, and I found a seat halfway, near enough to observe the stage with its floral decorations, some real, some plastic, and to hear the music being played on the electric organ by one of Brother Coleman's assistants, while another (both dressed in suits with a purple sheet like the wings of a starling, with diamonds glittering at the lapels) sang a preliminary gospel song in preparation for Brother Coleman's entrance.

The music stopped. The theater was filled. The two henchmen moved to guard the now closed doors. The spotlight played upon Brother Coleman as he walked upon the stage in his gold suit sewn with glitter to represent diamonds. He was God's Diamond Plan in person. He was smaller than I'd judged, with the appearance of the perfect stereotype bookie or pickpocket, with agile movements, an observant shifting and shifty gaze.

"O Lord, O Lord," someone cried out.

The organ began to play again and everyone sang.

"God will take care of you,
through every day
o'er all the way,
He will take care of you,"
swaying as they sang, hand-clapping, and crying out at intervals, Hallelujah, Hallelujah.

The hymn over, the crowd hushed, and Brother Coleman raised his arms like a priest and intoned in an impassioned voice.

"Give all you have to God. I'm not asking you to give *me* money, I want you to give to *God*. Come forward, all, yes, all," he almost screamed, "empty your purses at God's feet for God's sake; no matter how small your offering, God accepts it, God understands."

One by one the people came forward. Housekeeping money, bus fares, cashed welfare checks, rent, savings—the stage rang with the sound of falling coins above the mice-whisper of paper money while the assistant played a money-accompaniment on the organ and a tall dark woman in a shimmering purple dress sang a slow, prayerful money-song which, when the giving had ended and the two henchmen had collected the money in a glitter-wrapped container, as large as a tree-tub, changed to

"O love that wilt not let me go
I rest my weary soul in Thee
I give Thee back the life I owe . . ."
The audience, joined in, again swaying and clapping and shouting Hallelujah, Hallelujah.

88

Silence again. Another impassioned plea from Brother Coleman.

"You have held back. Look in your pocketbooks. See that crumpled note you hid from God, yes, I see it, God sees it, Give to God."

One or two, with faces ashamed, came from the audience and dropped the crumpled notes that Brother Coleman had seen with his God-piercing glance. Then silence again. The woman next to me whispered,
"It's time for the Miracle."

She frowned.

"It's late."

It was almost lunch-time. God and Brother Coleman would have to hurry.

Brother Coleman held up his hand to the audience.

"I wonder," he said, "if God wants me to help him perform a miracle this morning?"

"Jesus," he screamed, "can you hear me, Jesus, my sweet Jesus?" His eyes were closed. Tears trickled down his face, genuine, glistening tears. He tilted his head and looked up as if listening, and then he moaned and cried out, "Thy will, O Lord, Thy Will."

The crowd echoed him, "Thy will, O Lord, Thy will."

He sighed.

"We understand, Jesus," he said, "We understand."

He opened his eyes and cried, "We understand," and the crowd responded, "Hallelujah, Hallelujah. Praise the Lord."

"Brothers and sisters in Christ, the Lord does not will this morning that a miracle be performed. It is not the will of Jesus. The will of Jesus is perfect. We will pray, we will pray for the sick and the orphaned, the old and the poor. Let us bow our heads."

There was a hush, then a sigh as of disappointment, and a surge of movement in the ranks of the disabled who had gathered in front to be near the performance of the miracle and perhaps be part of it.

"Let us bow our heads," Brother Coleman repeated.

There was a long silence, then the organ music began playing the hymn.

"Have Thine own way, O Lord, Have thine own way,
Thou art the Potter, I am the clay,
Mould me and make me after Thy Will
While I am waiting, yielded and still."

The tall dark woman sang with the audience murmuring phrases now and again. Then, after another Hallelujah Praise the Lord, "exit" music began, a brisk march. The performance was over.

"Don't forget, brothers, sisters, two o'clock, be here for Jesus and the miracle."

Murmuring occasional Hallelujahs, the crowd moved on to grey, snow-filled Monument Street which, after the steaming warmth and the excitement and smell of the theater, seemed like the street of the hopeless with its drifts of tainted snow and slush and the dreary wind blowing the length of the street from the monument itself (with a giant George Washington standing upon a small stone building where, they said, if you paid a quarter, the guard would let you climb up the spiral staircase inside the monument and look out of a small door in George Washington's neck, at the view over the city) and the stately homes and apartments of the tree-lined square to the railway line, the rag shop and the mountains of rags with the children scrambling in it as if in a haystack in a golden countryside, past the jails, the Fortune Tellers, soul food shops, the medical supply store, the famous hospital where Brian had his Dyslexia Clinic, past the opulent furniture store where the windows broken in the recent riots had been replaced by brick walls with one small window remaining, displaying "his and hers" towels and pillowcases, past the barbers, the wig shop, the Roxy, the strip-tease club where you could watch porn movies and see a middle-aged strip-tease artist making her breasts dance, and throwing lace handkerchiefs (wiped between her legs) to the men in the front rows; past

90

the market, the stale goods bake shops, bargain stores, Five and Dime, the Salvation Army, the veterans, Volunteers of America, Purple Hearts, the launderettes with their half-dozen Speed Princess machines, mostly out of order, where the old man used to go, without any laundry, pay a quarter, and watch the water whirling around as the machine completed its cycle. For company. The dreary wind blew all the way, past the launderettes, the secondhand shops, to Pulaski Highway, on and on to the sick marshes of New Jersey with their dead swamp birds and rubber- and gasoline-smelling fumes.

I hurried home through the snow. I wondered what I should say to Mrs. Tyndall the next day. And that evening when Brian came home from work, I said, "I went to hear Brother Coleman today. At the Roxy. He's promising to perform miracles."

"That crook. He was run out of Washington last year. Promised to resurrect the dead. After this week's haul he goes to Miami, I believe."

I told him how I'd seen people outside the theater not knowing what to do because they'd given away all their money, including their bus fares and food money.

"All the same," I said, "they enjoyed themselves. They forgot the poverty and discrimination in the hope of miracles. It was warm in the theater, too. I enjoyed it."

"Ha," Brian said. He was angry. He had been brought up in one of those strict unsmiling religions where pleasure, particularly if it is accompanied by laughter, is a sin. He was a product of the New Zealand Bible Belt where parents administer with equal tyranny and force both the Bible and the Belt.

Later that evening Mrs. Tyndall's daughter phoned to tell us that her mother had had a stroke and had been taken to Brian's hospital, and Brian went at once to visit her, and when he came home I was still up, waiting for news. The house seemed to be full of guilt, intensified by the cleanliness of the bleach-smelling bathroom. And I'd forgotten to listen for the magic number, and Brother Coleman had failed to perform his miracle.

Mrs. Tyndall was very ill, Brian said. Speechless, paralyzed, nursing a carrier-bag like a baby at her breast, and not letting go of it.

"Nevertheless," he said suddenly using a dreadful doctorese, "her condition has stabilized but she will be hospitalized indefinitely and will in all probability die of cardiac arrest or another hemorrhage."

His language confused and depressed me as Mrs. Tyndall's "I'm very grateful, very grateful" had done, and my own "Are you sure you'll be all right in this weather?" Yet he was using the language as a means of giving the facts about Mrs. Tyndall; and why should one expect so much from words?

I have to cry out here that language is all we have for the delicacy and truth of telling, that words are the sole heroes and heroines of fiction. Their generosity and forgiveness make one weep. They will accept anything and stand by it, and show no sign of suffering. They will accept change, painlessly, the only pain being that experienced by those who use words, scattering them like beans in a field and hoping for morning beanstalks as high as the sky with heavenly commotion there, upstairs where the giants live.

I said nothing to Brian about his doctorese. He had his own reasons for using words, and we were living our separate lives, glancing at each other from time to time with clear intuition and acknowledgement of our littleness and powerlessness and our accumulation of self-deceits and compromises which we hated but could not help. I felt that he, as a doctor and counsellor, was more imprisoned than I who felt myself now to be on a relatively clear plain, living alone and apparent mistress of my every move—except in sickness and death and love where the losses and gains alone contain the chemicals which transform and transfix the memory and by creating "the light that never was on sea

92

or land" strengthen the power to marvel which, if the words are right, may make a poem.

That evening we could not help thinking of the sick and the dead, although we did not talk of them, and when Brian went to play the piano he chose first to play the tunes which held memories of our New Zealand childhood — "The Stranger of Galilee," "Jerusalem," "The Old Rugged Cross." Usually, we liked to parody these, remembering how everyone said "how lovely" they were, and as he played, Brian made faces out of habit but without the laughing references to the chocolate-box soft-centered feelings they (and kittens and bunnyrabbits and roses) inspired.

I thought of my early childhood in the south, of the kitchen at home with the coal range the center of warmth and light and food, the yellow flames gleaming through the black-leaded network of doors and dampers; my father in his chair in the corner reading the weekly *Humour* (I was amazed at the way he could solemnly read a book full of jokes and give only an occasional shout, as of anger, "Ha Ha!"); my mother constantly working, going from stove to sink to stove to table; the wireless, as we called it, playing the favorite tunes of Sunday—"Jerusalem," the "Old Rugged Cross," perhaps "Ave Maria," the one with "easy" music, while mother murmured, "how lovely" and father said, "screaming soprano." The warm moving flames of the fire, the smell of newly washed clothes airing on the brass rack above the range, the voice out of the old five-valve radio (the fewer the valves, the lower the status in the status-sharp world of our childhood), bought "on tick" from the big store in the city and sent all the way to our small country town where we had outgrown our "ticking" possibilities; a brown polished wood radio with many knobs, and green and red lights and a clock-shaped dial with the world stations printed on it. The rosy fire, the cooking smells, the peace broken only by the voice from the corner chair.

93

"The coal bucket's empty . . ."

It was useless to try to prove it was someone else's "turn" to get the coal, therefore the one named moved in a chill reluctant dream away from the fire, the wireless, through the scullery (cockroach territory) to the "outside," then through the wash-house, past the lavatory to the coal-house near the gaping hole which led to "under the house," where, racing under a double spell of ice and fire, against time, the "one" of the moment filled the coal bucket (a kerosene tin with a wire handle) or scuttle (fancy black helmet-shaped), returning to hear the last few notes of "The New Jerusalem" or "The Stranger of Galilee" or the "screaming soprano" presenting the arresting image of herself and the "Old Rugged Cross."

"I shall cling to the Old 'Rugged Cross' . . ."

As Brian played and sang I knew that his mind, too, was filled with early memories, perhaps less peaceful than mine, for his father died young and Brian's childhood was heavy with the responsibility always implied and often voiced by the colony of aunts and uncles, of being the "man of the house" with a duty to care for his mother and sister and two young brothers.

Mrs. Tyndall died that evening, still holding her shopping bag to her breast. She recognized no one. Her death was peaceful, for her, but for us it was powerful in its illumination of waste and the failure to account — in random telephone numbers and diamond bankbooks — the human debt and its payment. Baltimore seemed to be the farthest of cries from my time with Lance and his search for Yorkie Wynyard, and Blenheim with its altar-ranchsliders and alter-cloth of uncut moquette and wash-and-wipe vinyl.

Yet I smiled to think of Mrs. Tyndall, wherever she might be, making sure the thermostat was adjusted for her comfort, and no doubt turning it up; and I thought soberly that when I died I might still be wanting to turn the thermostat down!

94

memories my own, it is the television programs in the early days of New Zealand television, and the pop songs and records which have equal power to evoke the magical time.

Always when I see children whose hair and skin appear damp, (and not only children; such was the peculiar aspect of Brian's skin and hair) I feel they are living through a childhood climate that most others have forgotten. And when I see children beset by that other dampness of snivel and snot and intermittent tears, I remember the tide of misery that flows, forever in some children, in the holiday sea. And when, that cockroach time in Baltimore, just before I flew to San Francisco, Brian's nephew arrived from New Zealand to stay a week, and when I saw his damp skin and his pale snivelling face I wondered about him, half-child, half-fish, in that lonely sea. Lonnie was ten, the second child of three, with another expected, and Brian's sister, with Brian's advice and help, had arranged the visit to America as a special treat to give the "overlooked" child some attention. Everyone had worked it out and found the plan to be psychologically correct. Lonnie had been in trouble at home and at school with petty thieving, and vandalism; he was difficult to handle, they said; sullen, rebellious. Everyone said, just imagine his pride, coming home with tales about his grand trip to the United States! "He'll be able to dine out on it," Brian said, "until he leaves school. And after. And where can you find a less painful — such a *pleasant* — solution to a tricky problem."

Where indeed? Jet flight, crossing the line, skyscrapers, the land of Hollywood and westerns and the songs with the names, names, names with which Palmerston North, Marton, Foxton, couldn't hope to compete unless a spark of imagination, kindled somewhere (by Peter Wallstead, Margaret Rose Hurndell?) set the place alight like a bushfire. The Maori names — Wanganui, Waikato, Tuatapere, Taranaki—were more powerful because they were welded to the place by the first unifying act of poetry and not stuck on like a grocery label; nevertheless, the real triumph would be to set the spark raging in the mundane places.

And again, as people are impelled to live not only through their own lives, but through the lives of their children, the children of others, their friends, their relatives, Brian was anticipating Lonnie's delight in visiting America, his constant amazement, perhaps his gratitude and love, all in a warmth of experience that would melt away the sullenness and rebellion.

"He can sleep in the front room upstairs," Brian said. That was the room with the fur rug on the bed and the pop art woman dressed in pink standing near the window.

"She casts a shadow," Brian said, "and people think there's someone home."

But what will Lonnie do all day?" I asked. I knew that Brian wasn't free to take time from work.

"No problem. The neighborhood kids will be pleased to show him around. I've already spoken to Mose and James." Mose and James came to the clinic for reading, not because they were dyslexic but because they had missed being taught at school, and Brian gave them his time, unself-consciously, as one does away from home without the criticism and closeness of all other members of the national family. They lived near and often climbed over the wall into the tiny back garden where we had dinner now that the warm southern spring had come. They were often hungry, because, by the time each arrived home after the inevitable street-excursions of twelve-year-old boys, they found their brothers and sisters had eaten all the food. James, whose father was in jail, had a shoe-shine stand after school outside the locksmith's, while Mose, whose father was rarely in jail for more than a month when he was caught at the numbers game, worked sweeping and cleaning the radio shop after school. Mose who was brighter than James had a "yoking" arrangement with two other older boys: (one would approach a passer-by for the time or other information, while the two others remained in the background, and, when the moment was judged to be right, the two would come from

97

behind and "yoke" the victim, (with a length of rope or with their arms) while the third snatched the purse or wallet). Mose also carried a gun, a Saturday night special, and both were experts on the lore of the streets, and from time to time when his father was out of jail, James lived in the streets rather than go home. They were lively boys with a vivid sense of drama and a way of acting while speaking, imitating in voice and walk and gesture.

When Brian said that Lonnie would spend his time with Mose and James, I tried to imagine the milk-and butter-fed child from Palmerston North whose father grew (was it lilies? was it roses? or dahlias?) flowers for the flower show, roaming the streets of Baltimore with Mose and James and their friends. Brian, suddenly the parent, dismissed my doubts, "The experience will be good for him," he said.

Lonnie arrived, a miniature version of Brian, with damp pale skin and crystals like salt in the strands of his fair hair. Lonnie's dampness was accented by his runny nose and his habit of sniffing as if he'd just stopped crying. He looked dazed, afraid, and tired. His only luggage was what used to be known as a "Gladstone Bag," a kind I hadn't seen since my grandfather was alive—after he died, his Gladstone bag was put in the wash-house where it grew green fur and became a home for slaters and ear-wigs. I don't remember his ever traveling with it, yet when he grew old and came to live with us, it was his dearest possession. I saw the same pride and care when the old man living next door at Blenheim, refusing to buy an already-made carrier for his milk-bottles, stapled two columns of cardboard together with a handle from an old Heavenfield Mall shopping bag, and when he was taken to the Old People's Home he insisted on having his milk-bottle carrier with him.

Lonnie's Gladstone bag, clearly old, but recently polished, added to his old-fashioned appearance. His face was serious, like Brian's. It was evening when he arrived and he was almost asleep yet he managed to show us his collection of flight certificates and his Date-Line scroll.

"Isn't it exciting to be holidaying in the United States," I said, as a statement rather than a question, to which he replied, sourly, that his brother and sister were crossing Cook Strait all the way to Invercargill, and he'd never been to Invercargill.

"I've always wanted to go to Invercargill," he said wistfully.

"But *you've* flown on a big jet," Brian reminded him.

Lonnie sniffed, and looked coldly at him, "If you like that sort of thing," he said.

The next morning Lonnie appeared even more remote and damp at the same time, and said, without excitement, "O.K.," when Brian promised to bring Mose and James in at lunch-time to meet him, and, when Brian had gone to work and Lonnie and I were alone in the house, he sat as if waiting for me to suggest what he should do. He was afraid and every now and again he gave a big sniff.

Then he saw the television which Brian seldom watched and which he kept under the table away from the thieves who every five or six months managed to break into the house and remove all portable appliances.

"Can I watch TV?" Lonnie asked with eagerness and communicating his sudden pleasure by giving another big sniff.

All morning he watched the television, and when I suggested he come out shopping with me and perhaps look through an American five and dime store. "You've heard of the five-and-dimes?", he said, no, it was too hot outside, he wasn't interested, and there might be gangsters.

Then, noticing the portable fan in the corner he fetched it and switched it on. It was an old design, bought at the Salvation Army store, with large sharp blades only partly covered by a metal cage with widely-spaced bars, two broken.

"That's better," Lonnie said as the blades began to whirr. He flicked on the High Switch.

"It's hot in here," he said.

Then he looked around the sitting room at the heavy curtains drawn over the barred windows and the half-darkness lit only by the standard lamp beside the telephone.

"Where's the daylight?" he asked. "Why should I go out in the street? There's nothing to see."

"Well," I said unconvincingly, "there's the street, a street in U.S.A.!"

"But there's no real *outside*. Where's the *outside* like at home, with the lawn and that? And there's no inside either; it's all dark. And you should be able to see the outside from inside and not have to go unlocking and locking all the time. I suppose it's because of the gangsters?"

"Well," I said, "you have to be careful."

I agreed it was an effort to keep unlocking and locking. Even to go to the small backyard you had to unlock and lock and remove the heavy iron bar from behind the door.

"It's the city," I said. "It's not like at home."

"But why is it so dark in Uncle Brian's house?"

I explained by saying that after all it was the United States, wasn't it.

Later when Brian arrived with Mose and James, Lonnie was still in the sitting room watching television.

"I've brought Mose and James to meet you," Brian said, switching off the set.

"Hey, I was watching that!"

"Hi," James said.

"Hi," Mose said.

Lonnie stood to attention, looking constrained and a little frightened.

"Hello."

"I have to get back to work," Brian said. "I'll leave you guys to take Lonnie outside and show him around the neighborhood."

Lonnie drew back.

"No, I'll go tomorrow," he said. "Tomorrow."

"Come on," Brian said, taking him by the arm. "Outside."

He hauled the protesting Lonnie to the door and shoved him into the street and Mose and James followed, self-consciously looking "well-behaved."

"Get to see life in the U.S.A.," Brian called after them, and signalling me to lock up he set out on his way back to the Clinic.

Fifteen minutes later, there was a banging on the front door and peeping behind the rattan blind I saw Lonnie waiting to be let in.

I let him in.

"All they do is kick dustbins," he said. "And they set fire to a bagful of shit and watched when people stamped on it."

"Their life's different," I said, adding in a self-satisfied way.

"They're poor, you know. And they've never been to the beach."

"There's beach around here, isn't there?"

"It's different here," I said inadequately.

"One thing, there's no outside," Lonnie said.

He switched on the television and spent all afternoon watching, right through the mating and dating panel games, doctor and vampire serials, to the old Perry Masons on channel Five, and when Brian came home from work, Lonnie was still watching TV.

"Did you get out in the street?" Brian asked. "See something of the city? What do you think of it? It will do you good to get out in the Baltimore streets."

Brian was speaking as a parent, not from an image of an ideal parent such as a man of his knowledge might have in mind, but from a likeness formed from his own experience as a child. He was even using the parental language of years ago.

"It will do you good." Grown among the same crop as "It hurts me more than it hurts you," "Do as I say not Do as I Do." And his study of the likeness had been more

101

thorough, because he had been forced into the role, as a child, of being both parent and child.

"I'd rather stay and watch TV," Lonnie said sullenly.

"You can come to work with me tomorrow and meet the people at the clinic; and my secretary and her husband have invited you for the weekend to their place in the country. They've a swimming pool, and horses."

"I can't swim and I can't ride."

"Then it's time you learned."

Brian's voice, used to addressing students and others in tones of authority, did not change when his work was over for the day. Like Lance with his air of instructing and correcting, Brian had a permanent note of admonishment, and now there was a child in the house; there was an added stress of accusation, as if Lonnie was at fault simply by being there. Brian was clearly fond of Lonnie, and impressed by the likeness between them, yet the arrival of the "young" Brian aroused feelings in the "older" Brian that I sensed were related to Brian's fear for himself as a child and his anxiety to "do his duty" in a fatherless family. For a perfectionist like Brian, merciless in the working hours he imposed upon himself, and constantly complaining about the "lowering of the standard" of the work of others, Lonnie became a new kind of work; and in a house of prized furniture and carpets and works of art where wayward litter and destructive stains were at once removed, Lonnie became a new possession to be purified, cleaned and arranged. And living alone for several years after two early marriages, Brian was reluctant to be reminded of the necessary untidiness, the wilderness aspect, seen and unseen, of human life. He treated his patients with wonderful perception and compassion: they were not crumbs on his carpet; they were not his opened wounds or memories.

The next day when Lonnie went to work with Brian he did not stay long, and the secretary brought him home within an hour. At once he switched on the television and the fan. The whirring blades seemed to fascinate him and he began to put his fingers through the bars, withdrawing them as he almost touched the blades.

He saw my anxiety as I said, trying to sound casual, "You have to be careful with that fan. Your hand could be sucked in and sliced off."

This did not appear to worry him.

"You know," I said, "the way if you stand too close to a passing train you get sucked under."

"I know."

Of course he knew, I thought. It was another of the Great Dangers which mothers warned their children against. Watch out, you'll be sucked under, in, out. A powerful image to prohibit a move by erring children that succeeds now and again in enticing them to try their chances and that stays forever, an imprinted horror, in their mind. My parents tried it with me, and we tried it with our children, adding modern versions (planes sucked down, passengers sucked out of jet planes) to the trains, blades, quicksands, quagmires.

Taking no notice of my warning, Lonnie persisted in his daring game with the fan while I stood unhappily imagining his sliced and shredded hand and trying not to notice him in the hope he would stop. It was useless. I was as fascinated by his fascination. "This city's not really the place for a child," Brian conceded when Lonnie had left the next day for the place in the country. "He'll have fun at Marjorie and Don's place. Instead of moping and watching TV all the time."

"He's used to being outside."

"He could go outside here. Mose and James wanted to show him around."

"He's scared of them. Mose carries a gun, you know. A Saturday night special."

"It would do Lonnie good to get a bit of experience," Brian said sternly.

He could only have been remembering another time

when he was a child and his father had died and he was surrounded by those relatives pressing him into the responsibilities of being "a little man" to take care of the family; and how worried he'd been when everyone talked harshly of the need for "experience of life." He was not the sympathetic doctor respected and loved by his patients and admired by his colleagues; he was a stern dictatorial parent in command of an old-fashioned home and family with everything under control, in a fulfillment of the dream that others dreamed for him which then became his own dream as a small fearful boy with his father suddenly dead. I found myself being afraid of him as, with Lonnie gone, his sternness was directed to me, and his desire to clear the wilderness for ever showed as soon as he came into the house each evening, "Who—spilled, tipped, tore, split, left, dropped, lost, broke?"

When Lonnie returned from his weekend he was much happier. He talked freely about the horses and the swimming pool. He'd helped feed the horses and clean the swimming pool. There was no beach, like at home, but you couldn't have everything, and the horses were B-E-A-U-T and there was OUTSIDE.

Within the next few days his cheerfulness was replaced by gloom once more and he switched on the television and the fan and played with the temptation of being "sucked in." Then one afternoon he showed me the coins that Edward, the son about Lonnie's age, had given him.

"They're real silver dollars," he said.

And they were. Big shining silver dollars. I admired them and said how lucky he was to have them.

He replaced them in the small red flannel bag which, he said, had contained a compass for his birthday. There was a pink blanket stitch around the edge and a red drawstring. He carefully drew the string, watching with a hint of bliss the neat closing of the throat of the bag upon the silver dollars. Then he put the bag in the pocket of his grey shorts and kept his hand closed over their shape, over his pocket as if to prevent their escape. He still looked to be the gloomy, damp Lonnie but his misery had been eased or been paid for.

"I'm looking forward to going home," he said. "I don't like Baltimore."

A few hours later Brian phoned from work and asked to speak to Lonnie.

"That kid," he said to me, his voice angry, "he's stolen the Nathan's collection of silver dollars. It's a valuable family heirloom, a family heirloom and he's swiped the lot." I said I'd fetch Lonnie who'd left the television and the fan and was listening.

"Edward gave them to me," Lonnie said, looking at me "*You* know that."

I gave him the telephone. He took it and without waiting for Brian to speak, called out, as from hilltop to hilltop, "Edward gave them to me as a special friend. And Mr. and Mrs. Nathan said they wanted me to have them, specially, as a souvenir of America."

I heard Brian's answer to that. It sounded like, "You bloody liar." "They did give them to me," Lonnie insisted.

He began to cry then, and put down the phone and ran up to his room and when Brian came home Lonnie was still upstairs. I had never seen Brian so angry and stern.

"He needs a good beating," he said fiercely while I, fearful now, stared amazed at the transformation from a liberal doctor adhering to all the policies of love and care reverting to the image of the Victorian father, the New Zealand father with leather belt in hand waiting to whip his children as if they were racehorses.

"I think I ought to beat him," Brian said again.

He called up the stairs.

"Lonnie, come down here at once."

Lonnie did not appear.

"He's afraid of you," I said, entreating him. "You can't possibly mean what you say."

"Maybe not this time. But he's asked for it. By rights he should have a good beating."

"Oh Brian, don't be so cruel."

"I'm not cruel. The boy needs discipline. But I won't beat him this time, not if he returns the money and apologizes. How do you think I feel, accepting hospitality on his behalf, and he steals their family heirloom. A family heirloom! You go upstairs and talk to the boy."

I went upstairs and told a tearful Lonnie that Brian wasn't going to beat him, he merely wanted him to return the money and apologize to the Nathans.

Lonnie made no further attempt to lie. He admitted taking the dollars from a box on the dressing table in the Nathans' bedroom, and when Brian asked if any were missing, Lonnie said bravely Yes, he'd thrown some down on to the Nathans lawn to make room in the compass bag. Later, Marjorie Nathan, also fearful of Brian's anger, told me privately that the compass bag had contained Edward's birthday compass which they found also on the lawn with the rest of the silver dollars.

Until Lonnie, still damp and snivelling, flew from Baltimore on his way to the aunt in San Diego before his return to New Zealand, Brian and Lonnie and I spent unhappy days. The change in Brian frightened me in a way that almost persuaded me I was a child again, having committed misdeeds that required punishment, and Lonnie and I became conspirators, sneaking each other food and drink as if we were two children in prison. He told me about home and school and what he hoped to be when he grew up, and a day or two before his flight he began to talk of the United States as if it were his native land—just the right frame of mind for a triumphant return to New Zealand to announce what a wonderful holiday he'd had.

Lonnie flew on his way home. Brian once again became the "old" Brian or the "visible" Brian whose childhood, harbored within him, had escaped from him, slipped its moorings for a time. It was now back in harbor as surely as Lonnie and his new walkie-talkie and camera and University of Texas shirt which Brian, as the providing indulgent father had bought him at the airport, was safely back in Palmerston North with his family.

The week of the silver dollars remains, however, an unhappy memory, a glimpse of imperfections and of the tyranny of past experience. I used to wonder how people survived their childhood: I know now that few survive it.

17.

It was early southern summer. The house in Berkeley was waiting, the Garretts had arrived in Italy for their holiday, the super-cockroaches were laughing at the latest insecticide which Brian, not I, sprayed in the kitchen and the basement crevices. And where was my novel? I had briefly visited Menton where Margaret Rose Hurndell lived for a time, and I was interested in the "experts" which surrounded her, her work, and her memory. I've always been interested in "experts," right from my early childhood when, unlike many children I knew, I found myself to be temperamentally incapable of "collecting" and becoming an expert on whatever the collection might be—of information, stamps, photographs, matchbox tops, famous battles, rugby scores, dolls, salt and pepper sets. It was only since I began writing that I identified my own collection — the Manifold itself and all it contains. From time to time characters emerge surrounding an idea or a feeling or a dream, like creatures clinging to a growing vine, or parasites feeding for life upon their host. The *Watercress* family, the known experts on Margaret Rose Hurndell clamored for my attention which I was *paying* them in writing the novel. I was looking forward to the retreat in Berkeley, and I spent the last week in Baltimore trying to turn my attention from the events of my stay there, for one does not really "collect" substance within the manifold; it is the manifold which does the receiving without choice.

I remember very little about that last week. Brian was about to go on one of his conferences in the path of a round-the-world flight; and on the Tuesday (pleased to be arriving earlier and somehow "saving" a few hours) I took the noon flight to San Francisco where Grace Loudermilk (also about to fly away for the summer) met me with the key to the Garretts' house.

All I had experienced, all the stories I had read or dreamed came to me the moment I, a stranger, turned the key in the lock of the unknown house. I, Alice Thumb, sister to Tom, Mavis Postle, Mavis Barwell, Mavis Halleton, Violet Pansy Proudlock, Lorna Greenbanks etc., etc.

The Mexican medallion on the key ring glinted, not in sunlight for there was no sun that day, but in its own sparkle as I opened the heavy redwood door of the house on Grizzly Peak Road, Berkeley.

PART THREE

Attending and Avoiding in the Maniototo.

18.

My first impulse was to study the books on the shelves, and as I look over my papers of that time I find the notes I made: *Sister Carrie* and the *Natural History of Western Trees. The Diary and Correspondence of John Evelyn. The Compleat Angler. Science and The Educated Man. The Notebooks of Swinburne. Women in Love.*

The Works of Rabelais. The Golden Ass. Gise's *Therese. Pepys Diary. Barchester Towers.*

Let's Cook it Right; and (to make a rhyme) *West Coast Wild Flowers. This is Japan. The Paintings of Rembrandt. The Works of Chaucer.* Leatherbound poets locked in a row: Whitman next to Keats, Byron, and Shelley. *The Chance of Life. Of Human Bondage.* Mansfield Park. *The Letters of Van Gogh. The Thrones of Earth and Heaven.* Music, art, tapestry, modern, classical literature. Books from infancy and childhood; prizes, gifts. Books in cupboards, on shelves, on tables; in groups between blocks of redwood. *The Primary Structure of Fabrics, The Rise of the City, The City of Man, Great Cities of the World, Flat Woven Rugs from the Bosphorus to Samarkand. Textiles of Ancient Peru. Butterflies and Moths. A Lifetime Reading Plan.*

I found myself searching the bookshelves of each room to find the poems of Yeats, and realizing that there was no Yeats, I felt an unreasonable sense of loss. I wanted Yeats as an ally which is the word nations use now instead of "friend," implying a perpetual enemy.

113

A house without Yeats.

Oh, a wild swan or two and a paradisal Innisfree,
and age "old and grey and full of sleep"
all Fleckered and Blundened, Monroed beautifully
safe in proportion within a seldom-used anthology
all written before the time of the towering fury
when even the gentle dolphins not singing but gonging
like emperors, tormented the sea.

A house without Yeats.
The prisoners surrender, go quietly.
No surprise at the sentence — what is a day, a year, what
                                                    difference

but of indifference; and age a concealment, a verbal mask.
Hark the horns of Carmel are calling us to lifetime tenancy,
community sleep by a calm sea!
(They will sell this house and go soon to their chosen place
                              in Carmel,
the retirement home where there are suites and
              pleasant rooms, single and shared.
A medical center will they have there, a view of the sea from
                              the hill,
and a promise of ripe old age, if they are spared.

And they shall have company there in the large community
      room,
with color TV and parlor games; and a corner just to sit
and ripen as in a kind of pretomb home
where they think and talk about death and begin to
      welcome it.

They will sell this house and go soon, for their
              name's on the waiting list,

and they've paid a huge deposit for the suite with a view of
                    the shore,
where a golden age awaits them in a cloud of autumnal mist
arising from the gold decay of their deep hearts' ripened
    core.)

A house without Yeats.
A house with everything — books, geraniums in bloom,
    humming birds
at the throat of the morning flowers,
redwood trees, a patio, color TV, a piano with leaves of
    music (Largo, Oxen Minuet, Fur Elise)
comfortable furniture, masks, sculptured heads, paintings
                    and books on paintings.
Two large dictionaries.
House-trained house-plants; display alcoves, macramé
    hangings;
Mexican, Danish kitchenware; an Italian salad basket,
                    Australian ginger,
                    English conserves.

A house without Yeats.
Turning the pages of the old school anthologies
I search for the wild swans, the bean rows, the sleeping old
    men.

No rage. No towers.
Only the Garretts' lives demanding
I want a Shakespeare like the real Shakespeare
I want a miraculous marble table.
We have all, all, and "the agony of flame that cannot singe a
    sleeve."

And even had they not told me of their passion for Italy,
their book titles would have revealed it. I remembered the
English exiles I had seen in Menton, how they read and

115

reread the exploits of General Gordon of Khartoum, the
Life of Benjamin Disraeli, dividing their love between dead
famous generals and statesmen and neighboring Italy.

I love Italy, they say, the exiles, fingering the airmail edition
                    of the *Times*
(thin as the edible wrapping on their health-sweets),
I love Italy,
but where, except in England, can you find a good doctor?
The exiles, like the Garretts, are gentle people
with books and paintings and imagination
and money and books and paintings
and imagination and money and
arthritis, heart failure, dropped wombs,
enlarged prostates,
feares of cancer and of dying
far from home,
                    for where
except in England (and America)
can you find a good doctor?

The lovers of Italy sing in chorus,
The Italians are not like us, they let themselves go,
they dance, make love without shame
                    in daylight
as the cats and dogs of the region do
        howling among the beds of geranium, lavender,
by the walls of bougainvilia,
while we, lovers of Italy, have bodies whose flow is most
                    economical and mundane,
like soap-drops above the handbasin of a public
    convenience
or phials of medicine or droplets of insecticide
(domestic pets only, the antidote for overdose, milk.)

(Our dry riverbeds are beautiful

116

filled with memorial stones, tough gold-wired grass
sometimes called "everlasting," set
among fresh flowers upon the graves of love)

but in Italy — ah, Italy —
(we love Italy
bella bella bon giorno)
Give me my Giotto, my replica
my quarried artificial light
let us taste the "marble complexities" of the miraculous
Florentine
table!

I settled into the house, using Irving's study as a place to write, and sleeping in the adjoining double bedroom. After a certain amount of pacing in and out of rooms, inspecting, testing, exploring within the acceptable boundaries of human trust (not, as Yorkie Wynyard would have done, prying open locked drawers, but leaving the closed closed and the secret secret), I arrived at the state of being at home, and thus ready to turn my attention away from Grizzly Peak Road, Berkeley toward the Watercress family, now living in Menton to be "near where Margaret Rose Hurndell once lived." Unfortunately, as you will see, the house of replicas did not give up my attention gracefully, but contrived through events to compel me to return to it, and as writing is based on a carefully planned and controlled use of attention, I found myself beset upon, not knowing what to do, in a whirl of avoiding and not avoiding, haunted by the manifold, the replicas, and the originals.

There are some insects that carry a bulge of seed outside their body as the intelligence of the universe carries its planets and stars. A spider has its milky house strung *fragilely* between two stalks of grass; and so God has pitched his worlds; and we who are replicas and live in the house of replicas cannot exist until we have shaped what we have discovered within the manifold; and know in the repeated shaping that we are not Gods, and not avoid knowing that we ourselves have been shaped and patterned not by a shadow of light or a twin intelligence but an original, the sum of all equals and unequals and cubes and squares; the shaping inclusion; the hypotenuse of the entire manifold.

(There are some who live forever in the manifold; it hangs in their lives like a wild bees' nest full of the honey of assorted flowers, unexplored and untasted, yet attended, turned to, in an act of avoidance that does not touch or shape or change but may erase; others, on an individual path within the manifold finally escape from it, turning to themselves as original creators, thus intensifying their avoidance; and still others, within their individual patterning of the manifold, intent on avoiding its chaos, may, suddenly discovering themselves to be replicas, turn to the original, and realize that their ceaseless activity of avoiding and turning to and from has been passive with the center of activity elsewhere, like that of the motionless yet turning world.)

I felt that it was surely enough for me, then, to have the concerns of a writer only for the problems of attending and avoiding; and yet at the same time I hoped to get away with my kind of commuting between "real life" and "fiction"!

19.

When I had been living in the Garretts' house for only a week there was a severe earthquake in northern Italy, and, as one does with distant disasters, I wondered if anyone I knew had been hurt, and I thought of the Garretts, who'd be there now, in the north. Also, as one does, I imagined their dying, and the news coming, and what I should do.

Two days later the news did come. Irving and Trinity Garrett had died at the opera. They were attending the opera and were buried with the rest of the audience among musical instruments and half-sung arias that became, no doubt, the "steaming lamentations" that rose home into the harmonious blue of the Italian sky, resolving, completing the harmony of many lives. An elaborate way to say it, but it happened! Two From Berkeley Die At Opera. I found myself believing the news of their death simply because it was a coincidence that fiction would never have allowed, and certainly it would be forbidden by Howard Conway, and never used by Peter Wallstead or even by Margaret Rose Hurndell while even I, with the arrogance of an aspiring writer, might have rejected it.

The reality was that they were dead and I was living in their house. I'd only met them once and that meeting still haunted me with its replicas and replacements of people and objects, and I remembered Irving's hope of visiting Blenheim, the sister city, as the expert town planner trying to bring to birth his ideal city. Following the news, there were a number of phone calls to the house from former colleagues of the Garretts asking me to assure them there had been a mistake or they had misheard the announcement. Then I had a phone call from a lawyer, Julian Soule, who said the Garretts had told him of their arrangement for me to stay in the house. Before they left for Italy, he said, they had made a will which left their entire estate, including the house and its contents, to me.

At first I did refuse to believe this, for I do inhabit a world of fiction, and such fortune happens only in "real life"; in fiction such events have to be worked for and slaved over and then, usually, regretfully, left out of the story. Writers tend to be afraid to misbehave, and I am no exception, although I have a strong tendency and urge towards mischief and a panoramic defiance grows in my fictional garden, and, not as with Bannockburn Road in Blenheim, never mind the foul fumes blowing in from the public (and pubic) highways.

The next day I received an official letter from Julian Soule and a request for me to visit his office on Shattuck, next to the Pleasure-Treasure Supermarket. Already, though disbelief prevailed, my imagination was beguiled by the prospect of my living in a street named Grizzly Peak, just below Grizzly Peak itself where the mist from the sea had its second home and where, perhaps, the bears still lived in the wooded canyons and craggy hills. I was apprehensive, though, about the transition from guesthood or guestship to citizenship, for I was aware that such permanence does not receive the surprising forgiveness, nor hold the honeymoon quality and delight, of transcience. I knew. At home in my own country, New Zealand, as in a family, I can be harshly unforgiving with my vision unsparkled by a tourist glaze.

When I arrived at the office, Julian Soule in answer to my question, assured me there had been no mistake about the will. Nor about the deaths. The Garretts' bodies had been found and identified and would be buried in Italy.

"They were lovers of Italy," he confided.

There was a matter, he said, of summer visitors whom the Garretts had invited upon their return and who might have made arrangements for their stay. They were friends, as far as the Garretts had friends; and it might be a gesture for me to welcome them now for a brief stay and perhaps ask them to choose a keepsake. He had advised the friends of the tragedy.

So far, only the newspapers had used the word "tragedy" and hearing it spoken compelled me to recognize it. "The summer guests can visit at once," I said generously. "For their brief stay. If you give me their names and addresses I'll write to them."

I stopped, realizing that I had accepted the house without any polite struggle or astonishment or dismay and I was now the gracious owner (short of the completion of a few legal matters). "What about the taxes, utility accounts, and so on?"

"These are being dealt with, and if you prefer I can take them in hand until you decide what you'll be doing."

So, for his comfortable fee from the Garretts' estate I gave him charge of the regular household accounts. I might have been surprised at his lack of surprise over the will had I not seen enough of Californians to know that the diversities of the ways of life and behavior have brought an immunity to surprise: to Californians the world is blinkless. Had the Garretts left their home to a favorite pet, the lawyer would have been handing the key to a cat or dog or hiring a servant to attend to it, and even furnishing the house to its taste. I say a cat or dog. It could easily have been a king snake, alligator, mountain lion, raccoon (with so much provided each day for damages).

All the Garretts' key rings were the same Mexican design.

"It's a replica of the giant sundial near Mexico City. Irving and Trinity were keen on replicas."

His speaking of them by their first names startled me into thinking that perhaps he had been a close friend, and might even like a keepsake, and then I remembered the American use of first names, the semblance of the need for immediate intimacy in a crowded, lonely existence, and I couldn't help remembering how my parents and their neighbors who became lifelong friends, were still Mr. and Mrs. to one another in conversation and face to face, even when they grew old, in a shared endowment of privacy that can exist only perhaps in an uncrowded country.

"Were you friends?" I asked Julian Soule.

"I saw them quite often, as clients. We had them to dinner once or twice and Marian and I had an evening there, a good few years ago, when Adelaide was alive."

"Adelaide?"

"Their only child."

"Someone told me about her. She died at sixteen?

"Yes."

"Someone told me it was lycanthropy?"

He nodded.

I felt sick as I said the word and I wished I hadn't said it. I knew that chiefly because of the horror of coming face to face with it in "real life," it is mentioned only in fiction; but I have seen it, and know it, and I wrote about it in my book, *The Green Fuse.* I can't ever forget the thirteen-year-old twins I knew in hospital, the beautiful black-haired, blue-eyed children dressed in their dark blue and white striped hospital dresses made of the stiff material used for mattress covers; their bare feet swollen and blue, their arms and the upper part of their body bound in a canvas straitjacket; standing together on the stairs leading from the dayroom to the small exercise yard; and over the years I still hear in my mind the sound of their barking, yelping, whimpering as they made their bizarre canine gestures to each other and in their adolescent awakenings tried to mate each other, like dogs. And at night when the moon was full they would howl, above the turmoil of the screams and shouts and cries of the night.

Quickly I drew a deep breath trying to extinguish those memories that smoulder and that, I know, will never turn to dead grey ash. The Martin twins. I used to long to be able to help them. I began to feel that in my inheritance of the Garretts' worldly goods and knowing of the tragedy of their daughter, I was in some strange way easing the burden of the lives of the twins Tessa and Joan Martin, for they still lived, I had heard, in that hospital among the others whom the selective medical miracles had ignored; losing, as they grew older, yet one more reason to be loved—their childhood equation as pets, the Christmas years passing them by and leaving them in the unthinkable maturity of their "middle years." I can't explain how I felt I might be helping them except that they became a link between me and the Garretts, not only in being a reminder of Adelaide but in being another kind of replica, one human being of the other, and as this link they were at last of use, they were needed, they had strength—three attributes which, I guessed, few would ever dream they possessed. Their influence from a distance of space and time was immense and characteristically, for such is the way with influence, they would never know of it.

"It was hard to think of little Adelaide as human," Julian Soule said.

"But she was human."

"A likeness only."

I changed the subject.

"The Garretts have some interesting Italian pieces," I said. "There's a glass table, in mosaic, like one in the Uffizi Gallery."

"Their friends might like something like that, as a keepsake," he suggested.

"Of course. I'll let them choose."

"By the way," he said as I was leaving his office, "You are not as unknown to the Garretts as you might think."

"I know they read my books. *The Green Fuse. . .*"

"So it was the title of a book! I was curious. They referred to you as 'known through *The Green Fuse*.' I thought it must be a sorority, fraternity, you know."

He repeated then that the Garretts had no known living relatives, once again forcing me to discard my belief that everyone in the world has someone, somewhere, if only a forty-second or more distant cousin, a remote aunt, tucked away and unheard of for years but coming to light at a death, in response to the joint summons from honest grief, family loyalty, and the prospect of an inheritance.

I took a taxi from Julian Soule's office to "my" house on Grizzly Peak Road. I had been surprised at my resistance to the idea of giving away "keepsakes." I thought of my first real possession, or the first which I knew to be separate from myself: a golden velvet dress the color of jersey cows and chrysanthemums. I could wear it like a skin and yet remove it, and unlike the shot rabbit in the paddock, stay alive.

That evening I phoned Brian in Baltimore to tell him of the extraordinary events. I could hear the purring of the phone. No reply came, and I supposed that he had already set out for his conference in Europe.

20.

I soon heard from the four friends whom the Garretts had invited for the summer—Roger and Doris Prestwick of London, and Theo and Zita Carlton of downtown Berkeley —the messages from both myself and Julian Soule having crossed the two formidable distances—the Atlantic ocean and the space between downtown Berkeley and the Berkeley hills. The Carltons could come "anytime" and the Prestwicks would arrive in a few days. I did not see how I could refuse this service to the dead Garretts. There was room enough in the house. I could sleep in the small self-contained studio downstairs, one couple could have the main bedroom which had its own bathroom, the other could sleep on the convertible sofa in the study and use the bathroom opposite. The sitting room, kitchen, the large patio and the small flourishing garden would be common ground. I planned to let the guests fend for themselves, both factually and fictionally, as you will see.

A day or two later the Carltons drove up from downtown Berkeley to meet me and arrange for their stay, and when I heard them banging the carved door knocker (a griffin), I felt nervous. They too were nervous. I asked them into the sitting room and I guiltily tried to conceal a box of birthday candies which the Garretts had left on the coffee table and which I had eaten all of except for the one lemon jube lying on its side sprayed with icing-sugar and with my tentative bitemark showing in its moon-hollow. There was also a chocolate-shaped one like a foot within a frilled shoe.

I sensed the curiosity and perhaps the hostility of the Carltons for, after all, I was the stranger.

"We'd like to stay," Theo said, "for the sake of Irving and Trinity. They invited us, while we looked for a new apartment." I was startled by his New Zealand accent, as I had been when we spoke on the telephone.

"You *are* from New Zealand," I said.

"Ages ago. Zita too."

"Yes, I'm from New Zealand. And from Hungary."

"The Garretts were good friends though we didn't see them often," Theo said, glancing directly at the lemon jube which I'd not had time to hide. He had the kind of vacuuming glance that cleans up the view, or the locust ability to strip the foliage from the scene.

"It is strange," he said, when I had fetched the ice for their drinks, "to see you at home here when, by your own admission, you didn't even know the Garretts."

"Not as we did."

I was amiable.

"Yes, it does feel strange. Giving me the place to write in. And now the will. I've read of families being killed in one fell swoop and I often wondered, when there were no living relatives."

"We were quite close," Theo said. "Weren't we, dear?"

Zita agreed.

So far no one had mentioned grief, and although mine was general rather than particular I felt I had a duty to remind the Carltons that we were talking about the Garretts in the past tense because they were dead, they had been killed by an earthquake.

"They loved life," I said dramatically.

"Oh we know, we know!"

"They were great lovers of Italy," I said inviting the response.

126

"Oh yes, they loved Italy."

"And they've been found, identified, and buried there," I said.

"Surely, as they would have wished!"

"Surely!"

"There's already been a memorial service," I said.

"Here? So soon? Why didn't we know?"

"At the chapel in the retirement home at Carmel. They'd booked a place there, for later."

It occurred to me that I had inherited the place, the double suite overlooking the ocean.

"But they seemed so young!" Zita said.

"They loved life," I said again.

"Oh we know, we know!"

"Trinity was about seventy," Theo said in an ordinary accepting tone. He himself looked to be about sixty-five with curly white thick hair and the body line usually called "trim" with just a suggestion of belly flow in the small fleshy shelf jutting above his belt. Such detail is repulsive, I know, yet Theo was the kind of person who obviously paid attention to his body and sent out demand signals that others do so, too. He was a retired agricultural expert with soil and erosion as his specialty. His face was tanned from being in California and from working "in the field," and his voice was rather loud and insistent. Zita was much younger, perhaps in her early thirties or even late twenties. Her accent was Hungarian with New Zealand overtones.

"I think it's a matter of common knowledge," Theo said, "that I put Irving Garrett in his job. Not directly, but it was largely my influence."

He did not explain what he had done. Instead, he turned to Zita, gave her a quick embrace, and smiled.

"I even rescued my own wife from an unhappy world, didn't I, dear?"

Zita said nothing. She clearly adored him. They appeared to be very much in love.

"Irving and Trinity did say that if anything happened to them — they were joking then — they'd want us to have mementoes — you understand . . ."

"Of course," I said quickly, aware of myself as a usurper. "Our apartment is so poky. That's why we're looking for a new one. With Theo retired . . ."

"I still give lectures from time to time."

"And he's writing a book on erosion. Soil erosion. Trying to work in such a confined space in the apartment."

I sensed Zita's tenacity.

"You know the Prestwicks?" I asked, adding (and reminding myself of an elderly woman I knew in Blenheim who always identified people with their "place" — the Rotorua Wallaces, the West Coast Wilsons), "the London Prestwicks. Roger and Doris. She was a New Zealander too, I believe."

"We met them briefly in London. We were seeing Irving and Trinity off for Italy. Last year. They went every year."

"They couldn't keep away from Italy. They were so enthusiastic."

"Don't you feel that their house is more like a house where *young* people live? They had no children, did they? Just themselves?" Zita asked.

"Just themselves," I said. "Do you have a family?"

"Theo has three lovely children by his first wife. They're grown up now. Theo and I have no children."

"We have each other."

A smile, another embrace. "And you?"

Deftly I rearranged my huge inner glee to appear soberly in a sober light.

"I've buried two husbands," I said. "I have two children grown up and away. The Prestwicks tell me they have young children. They're leaving them with grandparents while they visit here. The day after tomorrow."

Both Zita and Theo looked alarmed, as if robbed of time. "He's a freelance journalist," Zita said. "And she was or is a teacher of geography. And they're staying here, in the house?"

"Of course," I said.

"Is there room here?"

I said there was plenty of room and I suggested they move in at once for their visit.

"For about two weeks," I said carefully. They could have the study with adjoining bathroom. "Tomorrow, then" they said.

"While you look for a new apartment."

That evening I made up the double divan in the study and the twin beds in the main bedroom and moved my two suitcases and effects down to the studio where I planned to live completely to myself. I had to keep reminding myself that it was my duty to welcome the guests and it amused me to think that had they been fictional characters I would have been far more demanding in my scrutiny of them and may have refused them entry to the house. From what I gathered, in the letters and in their conversation, each had the idea of writing a book or putting together material that would "one day" make a book, and I knew that Peter Wallstead or Howard Conway and others would allow a writer *one* indulgence of such a character, but not four at once! (Some time during a writer's career, she enters a wardrobe where she is invited to hang only her own clothing.)

That night I was too apprehensive of my role as owner and hostess to sleep deeply. I had bizarre dreams, one where my guests were fictional characters who brought two vultures as pets, named Past Perfect and Present Historic, one passive and seemingly at peace, the other aggressive, forever pecking and claiming attention. I insisted they get rid of Present Historic, which they did; then, unfortunately, Past Perfect died of overactivity, and my guests were left posed, like statues, frozen, leaning over the dead Garretts.

I woke early, in alarm. A faint grey light was growing

between the drawn curtains, a cold-underwater grey, streaked with cloud that penetrated the curtains and gave unwanted vision, to my tired stinging eyes, of the world outside, the cornered angled world, a geometry of danger. I looked at the clock on my desk. The London flight of the Prestwicks was due in two hours and I had promised to meet them. It was not yet time for me to hide away.

I drove the Garretts' Volvo (my car!) out of the carport (by the dew- and mist-wet morning glory) and set out for the airport, and I marveled, as usual, at the Golden Gate Bridge, although it was simply a memory-marvel, from the film San Francisco which I'd seen years ago, and where the swelling closing chorus inseparable from films of that era guaranteed in the audience a mixed feeling of surging love for human-kind and the longing despair of "I am yet what I am who cares or knows?"

I arrived at the San Francisco airport. The red and white wooden arm admitted me, my debt paid, to the parking lot. The automatic doors sprang open as I walked into the lounge. The Prestwick's plane had arrived. I went to where I knew they'd be, in the luggage room, infected by the endemic anxiety of luggage rooms where the crowd surrounds the revolving platform waiting to pounce upon suitcases and fearful lest they escape or remain unrecognized.

I saw the Prestwicks.

"Ours is blue," Doris was saying to Roger.

"Everyone's is blue."

"Not quite, dear."

"It's a matter of watching and waiting."

"Look! There!"

A primeval cry uttered at the sight of new horizons.

"See, high on the pile."

"It's sliding down. There's another."

"Got it. Watch out, Roger. There's the other coming round again." They had their luggage at last. Other passengers, their faces tormented with worry, dared not move their gaze from the revolving platform.

"It's all so confusing and giddying," Doris said, as I introduced myself.

"How did you know us?" Doris asked shyly.

I didn't answer. They were still not free of the airport anxiety. I couldn't say why I had recognized them.

During the drive to Berkeley they talked only of luggage, and I joined in, in a predictable way as if we read from the universal repetitive script of jet travel — stories of luggage lost, stolen, slashed open, recovered, traveling to unplanned destinations. "It turned up in Thailand."

As we began to climb toward the Berkeley Hills the two began to yawn (I also) and we were silent except for remarks such as "Isn't that fennel growing on the side of the road?"

"Fennel?"

"Yes, fennel. Look, a deer!"

In contrast to the shaven lawns of Blenheim with no grass blade out of place, and the carefully mown grass verges, Berkeley was passing through a "wilderness" phase where it was fashionable to let meadow grass and herbs grow as they pleased, and the wild creatures come and go in the gardens and on the hillside roads, with the deer and the squirrels having right-of-way on the road.

"Yes, a deer."

I explained that in the very early morning a troup of deer and fawns came down from Grizzly Peak and moved from garden to garden on Grizzly Peak Road, eating the vegetation. I knew that home in New Zealand the shotguns or the poison bait would be out at once, for the land is our savior and we insist that we have no partners when we exercise our presumed right to destroy it.

As we neared Grizzly Peak Road, having surmounted all the obstacles of jet travel and used up the familiar script, the Prestwicks spoke of the Garretts.

"We stayed with them only once, and they stayed with us on their way to Italy last year. They loved Italy. And this summer we were all going to work on our books . . ."

"Your books?"

131

"Yes," Doris said. "Roger is writing a book about the desert."

"And you?"

"Well . . ." She smiled shyly. "You know . . ."

"Didn't the Garretts have any family?"

"Nobody," I said. I had acquired a certain knowledgeable air in talking of them. "I always thought that people as awkward numbers always solved themselves into some kind of human remainder, but the Garretts were an exception. Nothing carried, nothing is left. They were alone."

Roger looked at me curiously.

"It's rather gruesome, our coming here after they're dead, but they did invite us. And as Doris said, I'm sure they would have wanted us to come."

"There are other friends?" Doris asked.

"The Carltons, Theo and Zita. I think you've met."

"We may have. At the airport."

"I remember it as a small house," Doris said. "Will there be room? Isn't it unusually angled and shaped? Crowded with artifacts and wall hangings? And a wooden mask of Shakespeare just inside the door to the patio?"

She blushed, as if she might have been thought to be checking the possessions.

"I come from New Zealand too, you know," she said suddenly. "From a farm, originally."

We arrived at the house. They watched as I parked the car in the carport. They exclaimed with delight at the budding morning glory, and the wisteria, at the attractive balcony overlooking the Berkeley Hills, the redwood trees, the white blossom tree where, I already knew, the hummingbirds never failed to appear, at noon, in a mist of suspended color and motion.

They remarked on the awkward triangular shape of the land. "Townplanners are not millionaires," Doris said, and I thought I sensed her New Zealandness in this, for where else is there such critical judgment of land, its shape, color, texture, fertility, and such extraordinary yearning among those who took over the land for a plot or section that is flat, bare, right-angled, like a large unusually accommodating grave? I too had been uneasy about the triangular corner section and the irregularly shaped rooms in the Garretts' house, for there was no rest in the shapes that they had chosen and therefore must have thrived upon.

I showed the Prestwicks to the study and waited to receive the Carltons, and when all four guests had arrived at last, I, in the privacy of my downstairs apartment, again pondered the topic of guests in the house, as opposed to guests in the house of fiction, and I remembered how in an early sewing class at school our first task had been to make a small hem-stitched towel which I, mishearing, believed for many years to be a "guess towel."

"We're making a guess towel," I told my parents.

The notion fascinated me because it seemed to suit the mysterious unexpected nature of guests and their relation to hosts, and even after having corrected my mishearing, I still marvel at the idea of the "guess towel," and at the richness of meaning within the words "guest" and "host," with a guest as originally a host, a stranger, hostis, an enemy, a host as a guest, an army, a multitude of men, women, angels; planets, stars; a guest as parasite sheltered by the host, the host a sacrifice and ultimately a blessed food. Thinking of the mystery, of coming to rest thus in the midst of words, and having them, because of their very transparency, block the light shining towards the longed-for view, I wondered if perhaps I should not abandon my role as hostess and return at once, either to Baltimore to be guest among the cockroaches and the crumbs on the carpet, or to my old home in Blenheim as guest of the history lessons of another land, or to my present home in Taranaki, a guest, as all are who live there, of the Taranaki mountain.

133

21.

A writer, like a solitary carpenter bee, will hoard scraps from the manifold and then proceed to gnaw obsessively, constructing a long gallery, nesting her very existence within her food. The eater vanishes. The characters in the long gallery emerge. I speak, however, of fiction. I had four guests. I wanted to know something about them. Their temptation to try to "tell all" was natural as they were within time and constantly fighting against it, whereas the characters of fiction have all the time in the world and beyond it and need not tell, deliberately, one secret.

Doris, red-cheeked as a geranium, short, almost buxom, with prominent bones, wide face, blue eyes, milkmaid feet, well planted. Roger, lean, fair-haired as an orchard.

"I was brought up on a farm in New Zealand," Doris said, "on the banks of the Rakaia river in Canterbury, always within sight of the southern Alps which were our true landmark, dividing, ordering, surveying, illuminating our lives. My sister Noeline and I spent our earliest years in a prosperous home in the days when cattle were the equivalent of golden treasure and sheep were as precious as white sapphires. I was too young to understand the depression of the thirties and the meaning of that day in late summer, after the drought, when my father loaded two suitcases on the carrier of an old bicycle and mother pushed the gocart with our clothes in sugarbags, and we said goodbye to Pansy the pet heifer who was in calf and without food, and to the sheep on the burned plains and the starving ewes in the home paddock, and we walked to the railway station (through miles of bluegum trees), and took the train to Christchurch. Our plan was to go to Wellington where we thought there might be a place for us and a job for father for, after all, it was the capital city where the government lived. (I remember the bewilderment and dismay of being told that the government was 'Old Coats.') Our mother's sister, Aunt Hilda, who had married the manager of a warehouse, would board us until we moved to the place they found for us in Thorndon. The plan, decided between mother and father, was for mother to take in boarders while father worked as a traveling salesman for Uncle Selwyn's firm, everything for the home, mail order a specialty.

"I always felt that some day I would write a book about our life in Wellington, starting with the time I rode in the gocart with Noeline and the clothes. I remember that mother and father had quarreled over whether to take the bedsheets, with father saying 'Other things are more important,' and mother, with doom in her voice, replying, 'It's the end, then. Without the niceties of sleeping there's no knowing where our lives will lead.' I remember also the color of the railway station, and I never see that color without being struck by a feeling of doom. The same color was on the boat to Wellington. (I remember having to wake up very early and being told, quick, look at the heads, and I looked at everyone on deck and all heads were turning this way and that and everyone was saying in amazement, 'look at them, look at the heads!') Even Aunt Hilda's picket fence was painted that railway color. I learned that it was a public color, that if ever you were surrounded by it you were not really at home, you were waiting for someone or something —a relative or a train or bus, or you lived in a house that didn't belong to you, that was only rented. Your life was in

135

transit, in a world the color of a wine biscuit or an oval arrowroot biscuit, the kind that is fed to people with a tender digestive system.

"Out in the country we'd never been short of food, but at Aunt Hilda's and Uncle Selwyn's, and later at the place we moved to, we had less, though enough. Mother was always home looking after us and the boarders, while father was away days and nights trying to sell things, and when he came home he was always drunk and there wasn't much money left from his pay. Noeline and I used to hide in our small upstairs bedroom and block our ears against his shouting and our mother's crying when he hit her.

"I tell you I grew cunning beneath my rosy milk maid mask. The change from farm to city was worse than any I have since known. The change of color, too, from green and drought-brown and grass-brown to drab grey, and the dark green of the Wellington hill-bush, a resentment, a mourning green. Nevertheless, there were distractions for us children — the wind blew often in Wellington, frolicking everyone about in the streets, and the clothes on the clothes lines and the smoke from the chimneys, tearing apart whole shapes and shadows, placing and misplacing every unanchored thing, while only great stones and mountains stayed unmoved. The wind blew through people and came out the other side with shreds of them and their thoughts flowing like ribbons in its path; and seeds alighted in their hair—one o'clocks, dockseed, sycamore windmills; while the wind coming around a street corner had a special fury, whipping off hats and filling them, like baskets, with leaves and flowerheads and dust. The Wellington wind was a kind that seemed to have escaped from the supervision of weather whereas our Canterbury Nor'Wester was part of the weather and kept its place, before rain.

"Sometimes there were the distractions of royal events: kings; and queens in blue silk coats holding on to their hats and smiling and saying

Our Great Empire
my peaches and cream complexion
your bloody wind that will topple me over and
our great Commonwealth of Nations which stands firm O
   Rock of Ages
except in frequent earthquakes . . .

"Noeline and I went to primary school and with the help
of Aunt Hilda and Uncle Selwyn, and some class scholarships, we went on to high school, the year the war finished.
It is perhaps not unusual for me to remember the centennial
exhibition, when I was eight, more than I remember the
war.

"We were girls growing up, Alice Thumb. Eventually
Noeline married and a few years later divorced. She is now
happily married, on a farm in the south. Our parents died
within two years of each other, of trivial diseases that no one
took much notice of at the time, while I, a teaching
graduate, met Roger Prestwick the young journalist sent
from England to cover the cricket tour. We married and
went to live in the north of England, on the outskirts of
Manchester, arriving there in January when the Common,
next to our bleak grey two-storied house, was scabbed with
snow and ice and the grass had the blood beaten out of it by
the wild winds blowing all the way from the Yorkshire
moors. The faraway sun could have been made of cutout
paper or tin or it might have been the shadowy bloodless
moon standing in for its absent reality, gone to the an-
tipodes to have fun, shining light and warmth. Up there in
the north I was reminded often of our shift from the Canterbury farm to the city. The grey streets that in Wellington
seem now to have been formed as the pigment of city
despair, became, in Lancashire, the color of the bereave-
ment induced by winter: people's faces seemed to be
shrunken with grief at the loss of the sun, full of hopelessness following the yearly assassination of light and color and

warmth. The tyrannical royal meal, once the golden warmth of the sun, was served day by day on a winter plate of ice.

"But what use is it to tell more? Here I am, with Roger, in Berkeley. Our two children, Kathy and Hugo, stay with their grandparents in London. From time to time I teach geography. One day, perhaps, I will write a book to tell my *complete* story."

I have allowed myself the indulgence of editing and in some cases embroidering Doris's story; I may have done this to compensate for my anger at having my view of the Watercress family suddenly blocked, replaced by the four guests and their compelling me to pay attention. If they stand in my fiction doorway like this, I thought, I shall come to treat them as such. But it was now Roger's turn to tell:

"I am a dreamer," Roger said. "And I dream of becoming a dreamer. An only child, son of an Anglican minister and a music teacher, I was brought up among good works and music, rebelling against both for a time by refusing to go to church and to continue music lessons, which saddened my father but did not appear to trouble my mother who tolerated my lack of interest and talent and concentrated upon her five other pupils who came to the house between four and five in the afternoon for lessons, with their shiny music cases and their tattered pages of music endorsed, like musical checks, with my mother's thinly penciled writing, Quietly, Gently, More Feeling, Listen as you play, Remember the Rests, Your phrasing!

"When my voice broke I had the excuse to escape from the role of reluctant choir boy at St. Matthew's. I spent much of my teens playing cricket, using it as my religion until, when I was seventeen, I suddenly became interested in religion after I had read that many boys in their teens experience religious conversion. In fact, my life seems to have evolved from a series of promptings from books and from the experiences of others and I have suspected that my given nature is empty as a ventriloquist's dummy. I'd read how the 'normal' boy of my age behaved, and I'd begin to behave in that way, and it was books which explained to me the facts of sex and led me to experiment. In a sense I have always been a shadow person acting the prepared reality: a man without secrets. In those early years, determined to experience this adolescent conversion I searched constantly for the 'vision' and imagined that the people I spoke to in the street were angels whom I alone recognized, and yet I knew this was fantasy for should I not know at once, as had all those others with experience of angels, all those fortunate others—ploughmen, herdsmen, poor engravers, apprentice blacksmiths, fishermen, carpenters, those with traditional access to the divine who were at the same time often the traditional comics—the Flutes, Snugs, Bottoms, Quinces, who worked with wood, cloth, mended bellows, the workmen who in our age would be the panelbeaters, mechanics, fish processers, plumbers, bank clerks? I, not so privileged, had only my imagining. Then, when I had scanned the earth and sky for angels, and had seen and heard none, I decided to proclaim my imagining as fact and in the end I believed my own belief and I was able, much to my father's joy, to return to the Christian faith.

'It doesn't come to everyone,' father said. "How proud of me he was!

"I have said that I am a man without secrets. I should say that my one secret from most people is the fact of my life's being the shadow of a conventional well-documented reality. I am what the scholars call a 'textbook' person. There are such people, detected often physiologically — their brainwaves flow in the exact patterns, their pulse beats the exact average, their cardiogram shows the working of a 'textbook' heart. Even my name, used mechanically in communication — 'Roger over and out,' 'Come in Roger,'

139

describes me. I am a 'model' freelance journalist with a wife, two children; successful in my articles on cricket, music, and religion. My book, *The Prestwick Report on the Teaching of Music in New Zealand* sold its small edition, mostly in New Zealand. I say that I returned to the study of music when I learned that music and cricket 'went together,' and following another of these seldom disputed tenets, 'chess and music go together,' I revived my childhood interest in chess. My return to music pleased my mother, as I think it pleased her when my life had passed through the acceptable traditional stages of childhood, boyhood, manhood — the three great Hoods. It was to please myself, however, and not in a way of fitting a pattern, that I became a journalist with an interest in unusual people, places and ideas, thus, in a roundabout way, abandoning the mass stereotype by turning to the individual and in the full circle of convention becoming a conventional eccentric. I spent some time in recent years in Europe and Asia and Doris and I accepted the Garretts' invitation to stay while I practiced an exploration of the desert. Perhaps Doris has already told you that I plan to go alone, next year or the year after, to cross one of the world's great deserts. You will admit it is a conventional, eccentric move. I've never been in a desert. I'll make a short visit to one in California to get a real taste on the tongue, after reading about, and seeing on film, and hearing talk, and dreaming and dreaming.

"My visit to New Zealand, where I met and married Doris, was a highlight of my life. I loved the green countryside, those forests that do not have the innocent infant green of our springtime woods with their clouds of silken aspen, misted oaks, birches with new light-green wet-skinned leaves. Our English trees do flourish there, at home in the shadow of snow-blue mountain peaks and glaciers and in the park-like gardens which each town takes such pride in growing and caring for, even if only (I may be cynical) in the hope that visiting royalty will graciously receive orchids and begonias from the hothouses. In a largely conservative extroverted country where life is spent outside, playing sport, mowing lawns, painting, sailing boats, trimming hedges, and inside, watching television and dressmaking, several municipal dreams are nourished, including that of the prize tropical blooms grown beneath glass, plants of the desert, all the spectacular vegetation of elsewhere; and thus each town harbors its climatic dangers, doomed frailties; the alien, the mistrusted, the envied, the longed-for and forbidden. How deprived those towns would be without their glasshouses! I remember writing an article for my newspaper, *The Begonia War*. About the rivalry between two towns and their decision to offer as royal prize or sacrifice either a floral clock or a prize begonia!

"Yes, Alice Thumb, I fell in love with that dark-foliaged bush which had for me an air of pain and melancholy, a spiritual grandeur which no one can ignore and which causes the population there to develop their lives in rebellious contrast — brightly-shouting, loud-voiced, many-musicked in the midst of continued trivia of the senses and a cluttering of spiritual and sexual hollows with electrically driven tools and household goods and gods. The forest and the land are so clearly the parents, the ancestors making their presence known, and what else may people do but rebel against a life of such dependence? In a land prone to earthquakes and volcanic eruptions, the concentration on the ordinary and everday, the visible, the representative image was like a means of holding the land in check as with a reins to prevent the great fires of ash and burning stones from being hurled from mountain to mountain, to prevent the monsters which move beneath the hills coated with centuries instead of fur, patterned with the prints of geological time, from destroying and erasing the inhabitants as if they were specks of dust or stray threads untidily disfiguring the time-woven cloth of earth.

"I saw these things, Alice Thumb, because I was a stranger and a man in love. Doris and I used to walk in the 'bush' as I learned to call it, and sit beside the green rivers that hold a permanent reflection of the land. I fell in love with the grass and the stones, those huge riverstones, white and smooth as pillows set in the summerdry riverbeds and the flowing snow-water, the green 'watersheets' 'textured' after the fashion, in a land crazy about interior and exterior decoration, for nature is never out of fashion, those sheets fitting edge to edge and beyond, flowing at times over the manuka, the tussock, matagouri-furnished room with the high ceilings painted in the blue identical with that used by the Florentine painters—the blue in that mosaic table there, in the corner of the sitting room. A replica.

"When Doris and I married, I would have preferred to stay in New Zealand. We now live in London, and since being there I've discovered something other than a world where people put on the 'common good' as a suit of doom. I began to think about the heroes, the religious heroes and heroines, the adventurous moon-visitors who, although so programmed and controlled that even their moon-landing speeches were prepared, who lived, like begonias in their nurtured environment, yet had moments of rebellion and assertion, triumphs of human behavior, which were misjudged misbehavior. And I began to think of the people who, refusing to be controlled by the organization of science, set out in small boats to encircle the world, to be alone with the sea and the sky, existing as human among universal elements without preparation of speech or breath or fragrant fecal sack or planned balance of computed activity. You may laugh at me, Alice Thumb, at the way I strive now to become the conventional rebel who yet wishes to act in the 'stereotyped' way by 'braving' the desert.

"I dream that in the desert, where sandgrains that accumulate without roots or obvious growth may blow in my face, with salt from dead seas, where the wind contains no promise or memory of sweet rain, I may find within myself an abundance of growth — not malignant, nor the type I have come to recognize as 'prize hothouse begonia,' but something of my own, a piece of reality that never had a shadow or a replica. You will say that such a dream is arrogant, ambitious, unoriginal, and of course it is, that what I hope to do will be a waste of time and money and may bring grief to my family and to those who will feel obliged to come to my rescue when, somewhere in the middle of the Gobi or Sahara desert I find I have to admit 'defeat.' But are there not always rescuers waiting to rescue? And the rescued always wavering between love and hate of the rescuers?

"I, too, will write a book. Another book. I know that our age has been propelled, blackmailed into becoming the Age of Explanation. I feel that literate people have almost explained themselves away. I use the word 'literate' as a fact, not a judgment. At first, you remember, Alice Thumb, it was our anxiety, our unease which was explained away, but in the process, we ourselves have been disappearing. The efficiency of our explanations is like that of the insecticide which reduces the insect to a crumbling shell.

"Yet here I am, even now, explaining, here we are telling our story, there is no end to it in the literate world, explaining and telling, propagating and admiring the tongue blossom, 'day by day uttering speech and night unto night showing knowledge.'

"Then why is each of us so diminished by the resulting fruit of this tongue-blossom?"

23.

"I am the old man among your guests, Alice Thumb," Theo said. "When I look in the mirror I see my sun-tanned skin, my glossy white curly hair, my fine athletic body, and you will notice my habit of making some move or gesture to draw attention to my body, to let it and not I announce that my years are far fewer than sixty-five. I have always been proud to be a man, and although I do have liberal views, I despise unmanliness. I insist that, although I like to watch the tide of knowledge overtaking my lands and islands of opinion, there are some areas which it cannot touch or change, and we know that when the tide of knowledge cannot submerge opinion in its cleansing flow, then those unreachable lands and islands remain part of the Empire of Prejudice. This habit of metaphor, by the way, is yours, Alice Thumb, Violet Pansy Proudlock, not mine.

"I, too, am a New Zealander, now an American. My parents had a corner shop in the inland holiday resort of Blenheim in the early 1920s. It was a pleasant place, with native bush and orchards and farms and holiday beaches. And mosquitoes. And in summer you couldn't hear yourself speak for the din of the cicadas and crickets. And there was a ferryboat across to Auckland city, and on Sundays we'd either cross in the ferry or walk through the bush to the beach at Birkenhead or Takapuna. We were poor and business was slack, and we were always on the verge of bankruptcy, yet mother and father (who came home un-wounded except for the usual shrapnel relic from the first world war) were forever optimistic about making a fortune, and each evening when the takings for the day were set on the kitchen table to be counted, beside the feeling of doom that lay there, almost visible, as a kind of auxiliary payment which we had to accept as if it were legal tender, there was a wild mad hope which spurred my father into thinking he was a great financier. Since those days, money has obsessed and depressed me: I like to get it, then to get rid of it.

"I was a clever child, helped by scholarships to continue at school and university where I studied agriculture specializing in soil science, later lecturing to training college students, then becoming the principal of the training col-lege in Dunedin where I began to realize and put into practice my talent for directing the lives of others. It has seemed, at times, that I was born into vicariousness, that I can achieve many of my ambitions only through the lives of others. I imagine that the original of such a character may be Jesus Christ. I, however, am an atheist.

"I met Zita in Dunedin when I was principal of the training college and she was a student, seventeen years old. You can imagine the scandal. I was fifty-seven then! She was passing through an adolescent unhappiness and I res-cued her from suicide. I was already married and one of my sons and a daughter were students at the college. I could write a book about that time in Dunedin—the gossip, the disapproval, the waiting for the divorce—I lost my job as principal. We married and came to live in California where I lectured in soil science, retiring two years ago, only just eligible for a pension. As you know, I'm now writing my book on erosion. Zita and I are very much in love. She is often mistaken for my daughter. She is mine; I rescued her; I deny her nothing. Let any unmarried or married man come to our apartment and smile at her and I am ready to kill him. I discourage her acquaintance with any other man."

"When you grow old, darling," Zita says, "I will take care of you."

"We both enjoyed the company of Irving and Trinity Garrett, partly because they were so absorbed in their work and art and craft pursuits that all they left for others was a kind of neutrality which enabled them to accept without judging the lives of others. They have been described as 'colorless,' an unusual description for two who decorated their home in what I, who am illiterate in color, I admit, think of as 'advanced' colors, an avoidance of bold primaries and a seeking out of subtle mixtures which I think it needs taste and experience to like; there's also the question of whether one will yield to or rebel against the assumption that these colors are 'better' than 'ordinary' colors. That green drape over the sliding door to the patio is, to me, the color of cowshit. Those cushions between grey and brown, remind me of rat poison. Give me, any day, that magnificent blue of the mosaic glass table, the replica—you say—of that in the Uffizi Gallery. I'm too old to recline on cowshit and lean my head on rat poison. My likes and dislikes are fixed now, and dear Zita, who I have educated to be literate in wifeliness, pampers me by her knowledge of them. When we have found our new apartment, I guarantee that we shall be the happiest couple in California."

24.

"I'm the youngest guest, Alice Thumb," Zita said. "I'm twenty-five. Let me tell you something of my life. I have a vivid early memory of eating a meal of boiled shredded cotton flannel mixed with one mashed potato, as a soup which served our family for our one daily meal. And that was some years after the end of the second world war, in Hungary. I remember terror, and lights blazing, and being in a camp with my parents and brother, waiting to be chosen, approved of, by the New Zealand government, which said it was willing to 'take' some of us after the 1957 uprising. Everyone said you had to be extra clever and beautiful and good and healthy to get into New Zealand, therefore most people did not try, so many of them were sick, with limbs missing, and sores, and lice, and you weren't approved of, if you were sick or had limbs missing or were dirty; and some who'd been angry and violent were also not wanted. Therefore, it was only the quiet ones, like us, who were chosen, with all our arms and legs and cheerful smiles and clean hands and face and hair (everyone said you had to like baths and washing, and I remember mother's joy when it was reported by the interpreter that one of the New Zealand officials had said our family was 'spotless.' It was translated as not having measles, but later we learned that it meant not being stained with blood or beetroot juice). We did feel sorry for the poor old people, some of whom were

147

deaf or blind and not wanting to wash because not washing kept you warm in winter, but we didn't have time to feel too sorry for them, we were so busy practicing to look adaptable and smiling and intelligent. Father was skillful at teaching us. He knew English, too, and taught us English words and phrases and when to say them, and especially to say them when the New Zealand officials were visiting the camp with their briefcases full of notes about us, and their judging faces. Oh, we had such dreams of New Zealand! What a clean, healthy, good, beautiful smiling country it must be, with only clean, beautiful, smiling, good, healthy people. It sounded like Paradise.

"We came to New Zealand by ship. There were lessons in English and my brother Josef and I were soon speaking more English than Hungarian, and our father too, for it was his English that had helped him to be chosen. It would enable him to 'fit in,' they said. The New Zealand aim was to have people who would 'fit in' readily and painlessly (painless for those already there). Like invisible mending. Or like an insect that moves to another tree and is given a new camouflage and told, stay on that bough, blend, and all will be well. Pretend you are not there! On board ship they taught us to sing 'God Defend New Zealand,' 'God Save the Queen,' 'Danny Boy,' and 'Come O Maidens Welcome Here, You in All the World So Dear,' which they said was a Maori song and we would learn the Maori later. Perhaps you do not know what it is like to learn English? Let me remind you:

I thought I sought a bough.
I fought. I fought through the night.
It was a tough fight. I lay on my couch,
I coughed all night, surely it was enough, all, all was
	known,
sea, sky, and crowing clown of light,
the morning sun crawling all undone upon the stone
and I, one, the world gone, living, surviving, all alone!

148

Moved by love I drove my steed
a steady pace. I fed
my love bread which I did not knead
upon a hearth of stone colder than the earth
and now beneath the bough my love whom I need is dead
while I live warm, come to no harm, trying to find
the mystery in the mysterious storm-wind
yet grieving to give good food to the dust and the worm,
asking what has occurred
in this May maze of treacherous word.
Teach me, I hope you may.
Save me. Have pity.

"When we arrived in Wyndham, New Zealand, we were met by members of the local council who had been working for a year toward welcoming us and who had given us, through contributions from various local organizations (the churches, the Wolves, The Bears, the Primitives, the Buffaloes) a house set in a plot of land that already had a garden with vegetables, flowers, a closely mown lawn, and a wooden fence painted dark brown. The house was fully furnished with food in the larder, and the day we arrived there was a fire burning in the fireplace, with wood and coal ready for restoking. There was even a clothesline in the back garden, and at the gate a small wooden house, painted red, for the mail. Everything was polished and shining and clean as we imagined it would be in New Zealand. There was a job for my father, an expert printer, with the local newspaper and although he found it hard at first, he soon recaptured the use of the English he had once learned, and, with the help of the head printer who was soon to retire, he grew familiar with the printing of English letters and the strange sounding local names.

"After Josef and I had been at the local school for a year we were both speaking more English than Hungarian. Also, we preferred not to speak Hungarian because it made us feel strange, and we sensed that others disapproved, and fancied that we had secrets from them and were talking about them. Mother was the only one who could not seem to learn English, and she still talked in Hungarian to father, and then, gradually so that we did not notice it happening, she began to be silent, not speaking at all, and once when father had to take her to the doctor for some ailment the doctor suggested that she was mentally unsound and should be in a psychiatric hospital, but we knew it was only her fear of the language. Rarely, I would hear her speak at night, and recognize the murmur, and the intonation, and, sometimes in the confusion of the night and sleep and dream, I'd think we were still in the camp waiting to be chosen by the spotless New Zealanders, and the conversation of my parents was the planning of what we would wear, do, say, the day the spotless people came to choose.

"Josef and I and some of the other children used to play a game of being chosen, and some would be the choosers and those waiting to be chosen would sit in a row on the ground, and, when the choosers appeared, would spring to their feet and start smiling and saying English words and appearing very intelligent and healthy, while the choosers walked up and down whispering to each other. I thought it was remarkable that when we were at last in New Zealand we girls used to play a choosing game (in fact the choosing games were without end) called Oranges and Lemons and either your head was chopped off or you had a reward and had to choose a treasure, a ruby necklace or a silver thimble. We played the farmer choosing his wife, too, and the wife choosing her child, and the child choosing a toy; and in all those games I had, now and then, a sick feeling of apprehension as if I were back in the camp in Austria.

"Our Wyndham childhood was happy, but it was also lonely. During the first two months of our stay in Wyndham, reporters came to see us and photograph us in our new home, and neighbors brought baked pies and cakes, and fruit, big polished red apples; and pears; and everyone smiled at us in the streets and in the shops; and the priest talked about us in the Sunday homily; and then, without our noticing the exact moment, yet it happened quite suddenly, people left us alone, and no one except father's new friend, the printer, and the priest, came to visit us; and the people in the street were too preoccupied to smile.

"We wondered why. Perhaps we had done something wrong or made too many mistakes in English; yet we knew they were proud of us, for the official choosers had talked about us over the radio, saying how spotless we were, among those who fled to Austria, and how we'd been *filtered* (like pure drinking water) first by the officials from London. Perhaps it was time for us to become invisible like the insect newly camouflaged on the new bough of the new tree? Or it may have been our mother's inability to adopt the new language, and her silence.

"During that year several more immigrant families came to that district, but the town did not give them the same attention they had given to us, the first chosen family. Many of the others were lonely from the beginning of their stay, for they'd been to other countries before New Zealand that said generously, 'We'll take some, say, half a dozen families of the screened and filtered,' and they'd gone to a camp in Otago on a plain called *Maniototo* where they were 'processed' and taught to sing 'O Danny Boy the pipes, the pipes are calling; From glen to glen . . .,' 'God Save the Queen' and 'Come O Maidens Welcome Here.' When some of the immigrants had complained about conditions at the camp, the people of the district began to question whether it was worthwhile helping refugees who were ungrateful, especially as they had been carefully chosen and were said to be the *cream* of the refugees, and everyone knew how important cream was; it was almost holy. To dare to criticize your host country! For New Zealand was our host, the kind, discriminating host, and we were "duty-bound" to be the respectful, grateful guests.

"Guests eventually go home: we stayed, subtly transforming ourselves into hosts. Mother grew thin and old and grey, with a hungry expression which she had not shown through all the hungry years; while Josef and I flourished almost as if mother were offering part of herself as food which we, in a matter-of-fact necessary way, accepted and consumed.

"After leaving school Josef found a job on a farm, and when he married he was able to get a small farm of his own. I went from high school to training college, and Theo has told you my story from there. I remember that by the time we left Dunedin, Theo and I had one real friend, a lecturer in Latin, whom we had not, at first, known well, and indeed had avoided as she gave the impression of being a social bulldozer, yet she, Gladys, invited us to spend our last few days in Dunedin at her home in Roslyn overlooking the harbor and the peninsula. On our last day we drove out to the end of the peninsula to see the Royal Albatross colony. That visit is a story in itself. Or a book. One day I will write a book.

"And now, Alice Thumb, we are here living in downtown Berkeley, and looking for another apartment. We have no children of our own because we want only ourselves, and Theo says, in fun of course, that I am his child. He likes to buy me clothing and jewels, to decorate me, as the chosen child in the game is decorated with treasure in a world of fantasy where nothing is really lost or hurt or killed. He likes to remind me and others that he has rescued me: he is a great rescuer. He once rescued a student, Al Tithel, from drowning and last year when Al became head of the art department at the college, Theo wrote him a long letter congratulating him and telling him how he had followed his career with interest since that day, many years ago, when Al was trapped in the surf at Brighton and would have been drowned had not Theo rescued him. Theo has a *stake* in everyone he has rescued, for in a sense he may claim to have resurrected and recreated them and as they owe their lives

152

to him, he is indirectly responsible for any good fortune they may have. Naturally he does not take responsibility for misfortune—the bond of the original rescue includes only the good. I'm not being cynical in saying this. Theo is a *good* man, but having a *stake* in a person (and allowing for all the peculiarities of the English language) does imply that the rescued has drunk one's life-blood, and that where one has given life one may have the right to give death by having a *stake* in the person's heart. (You see how strange it is that language in itself may be a force to prompt behavior.)

"Yes, Theo is a good man. He has made enemies — rescuers are inclined to make enemies, often of those they have rescued. He has many friends. And when we find an apartment of our own, instead of renting as we have done for the past five years, our lives will be entirely happy, rescued and rescuer together. He will write his book on erosion, and perhaps I shall write my book, but mostly I shall look after him as he grows old, while he will continue to be my rescuer. We need only each other."

25.

If it hadn't been for the practice known as The Great Californian Confession (the G.C.C.) I might not have gleaned so much about my guests. At that time, as a requisite of the Age of Explanation, the G.C.C. was at its peak, especially in California, and even Brian, usually taciturn, had stayed at experimental centers where guests, stopping only for sleep and food, poured out their hearts to one another, like sacks of coal (which burns) or wheat (which sprouts), and when their hearts were emptied they did indeed appear like empty sacks and may have been as desolate had not the owners or carriers realized that sacks are of the material which, in other circumstances, can be woven into fine linen, embroidered with bright flowers, birds of paradise, fish, castles, places and symbols of an age of imagination.

I retreated to my studio where I made the following notes:

I, Alice Thumb, delve more deeply than I have known.
I fly, "bat's back" etcetera, epochs and ages gone.
Doris, the blooming one, has she no extramural desire?
Doris teaches geography. She says, "My husband is fertile,"
             what prompts him to desire the desert
except the longing for what he has not.
I am a geranium, colorfully bred. He seeks

a vegetative pallor, the desert and chaparral,
a contained thirst; he seeks to be a saguaro bursting
filmy white corollas into their "full-seeded crimson"
though this he does not know. He sees only the pallor,
                                            always the pallor.
Roger, Regal horned lizard. Antelope jackrabbit.
a blossoming paloverde, a venomous gila
a sandsnake swimming in sand?

A cactus forest? And I, a cactus wren? A mourning dove
protected by the spines of the cacti? a gilded flicker,
                                sparrowhawk,
purple martin flycatcher
A saguaro forest? Granite, black lava,
the sandstone long eroded.
A chuckwalla
a joshua treeringtail
roserunner?
costa hummingbird of the mountain desert?
He will know (as I do, teacher of geography, name the
                deserts of the world, their flora and fauna)
that what seems to be may not be so?
A man who yearns for the desert, for the company of
        nothing
may grow thorns, put forth crimsom blossom, feast on his
                own stored blood
after the blood-rains of each season fall from whatever sky
                he lives under
defending the sun's intensity
its privilege of burning
its gift of cautery,
the eschar that may be God.

Yes, I am Roger with the English name, the Read-You-
Over and Out, of space, moonwalks, promised planetary
    tomorrows.

Roger, the translator of clichés into rules to live by,
my life woven of commonplace beliefs into which I work
                              the pattern of myself.
The wilderness, the desert—why are they not crowded with
                              pilgrims?
In the heart of one hundred and twenty in the shade
I may untangle the thread of person, saint and God.
I will be the mad Englishman who dreamed
(traveling in a God-accepted country) that a rattlesnake
                              would be kind to me,
the cactus thorns are the buds of appleblossom,
the sandstorm is the cool ocean spray
from an enveloping cool sand-sea.

I, Theo, write my book on erosion.
I learned as a child of its threat and horror. I used to
      go to Central Otago in my home country.
I saw the rabbit-made landscapes, their deserts of golden
                                          warrens
where they lived sleeping on deep pillows of bullion
in crumbling palaces that were pathways to and from the
      sun.
Today, in memory of rabbits, there are men and boys (even
                  a town) named Bunny, proud of the name
while children sleep embracing the soft-furred rabbit
                                          toys,
the once kings of the golden kingdom.

I learned the coastline of my land by heart. In waiting-places
my fingers traced it lovingly in my mind
gently following the great *bites* made by the sea's perpetual
                              hunger.
You know, perhaps, that I had planned, with Irving, a study
                  of the land in Blenheim,
once my almost-wilderness home (we lived on Windy
      Ridge Road;

I went to Windy Ridge School now the El Alamein High
    School)
now the battle city, our twin,
with the scars showing.

Ironic, the Garretts' death by earthquake,
their erosion, their erasure from the earth.
Once at a cocktail party for town planners someone asked
    me
instead of the usual
How do you feel about the political situation?
How do you feel about foreign policy?
What do you think about the plight of the world?
(Or, have you heard of C.'s divorce?,
What do you think of K. tonight?)
How do you feel about the Earth?
(The Earth, like the Great Californian Confession, was in
                                fashion.)
I, Theo, am haunted by three things:
my love for my wife, my past rescues and the rescued; and
        the erosion of the face of the earth.
Not its movement, displacement, reforming, but its
            ulceration and destruction."

Although the above notes may have incurred the disapproval of Howard Conway, Peter Wallstead and others,
they are part of trying to transform the Great Confession
into the Great Shaped Confession. The guests had "settled." They occupied the Long Gallery. They worked out
their domestic arrangements — cooking, cleaning, shopping, caring for the garden and the house plants (the
philodendron and the ti-plant). And I, secluded downstairs,
as Alice Thumb, Violet Pansy Proudlock, Ariella, or even
an ordinary widow with a shopping bag in each hand and a
life (no matter how many husbands have been buried)
broken in half, found it impossible to deal with the fictional

157

Watercress family while the fact of the four guests persisted.

I don't believe that I had thought seriously about the responsibility in writing. I thought of it as a take-it-or-leave-it occupation, with words dropped along the way, characters created and cast aside, ideas left to smoulder, landscapes trampled, defaced, eroded, for after all it was "only fiction," "only" in the imagination where power is limitless, private, the concern only of the one who is imagining. I knew also that a writer evokes characters at her peril and that ideas which burst into flame and burn everything within sight and touch an understanding, will not be extinguished easily. I suspected that I might have to "pay" for my casting aside, even temporarily, the Watercress family to direct my omniscience toward my four guests, although the peculiar fact is that, had I not written two books which the Garretts read and which influenced them to bequeath me their home, I would not have these four guests to distract my attention, and, inevitably, at the cost of self-erasure (which perhaps vindicates Tommy and his approach to the Blue Fury) treat as fiction.

The guests now had about two weeks left in the Garretts' house. I had asked them to choose a keepsake. Several times I phoned Brian in Baltimore and hearing only the purring of the telephone, which no one answered, I supposed that he had really gone to the conference in Europe. I was anxious to know what he thought about the recent happenings—the earthquake, the inheritance, the guests, and although I tried to remember, I found that my memory of that last week in Baltimore had faded completely, and that I, who fancied myself as, among others, Violet Pansy Proudlock, ventriloquist, was myself a mere talking stick or pocket head in the entertainment arranged by Reality.

PART FOUR

Avoiding, Bound by the Present Historic.

26.

First, there must be a note about the weather. In a country like New Zealand where there is a richness of sky and the moods of the day are accessible to anyone, weather is intensified in importance, and as an aspiring writer I am always sympathetic toward those novelists who are forever criticized for "writing weather reports" at the beginning of each chapter. I make no excuse for writing about the weather. Every country has a neighboring sea and land mass which endows it with immigrant seeds, birds, people, viruses, vices, dreams, and weather. Here in New Zealand the atmospheric gifts that can't be rejected come mostly from Australia—dregs of storms, stale heat waves, or from Antarctica—snow-filled winds and storms. In France the sirocco begins in the Sahara, the mistral blows south from the Massif Central; in North America the weather arrows point from Canada and the north, and Mexico, or the east of the continent becomes the aftermath of the west, the west of the east: it is all elsewhere. The heat wave that struck California during my stay was the result of warm air flowing from the desert, making the desert a double focus of attention, for Roger talked of little else but the visit he would make, spending "two or three hours" in his "first" desert. He was like someone whose goal to write an epic had touched with glory and promise his announced attempt, as a way of beginning, to complete a rhyming couplet.

The memory of the time ("it is not enough to have memories. One must be able to forget them and to have vast patience until they come again") has the quality of a mirage seen within the heat wave, and as I watch it I note that in the house of the dead Garretts there is a competition for perfect living, to be judged by the dead Garretts. The Carltons and the Prestwicks look on themselves as truthful, intelligent, tolerant, liberal, applying to themselves the fashionable adjectives of approval, yet one may calculate from the number of times each remarks, "We're very happy together," "We're very much in love," "We have a perfect marriage," that all four are oppressed by private unhappiness. It is easy to believe the declarations made by Theo and Zita when the catapult of Californian confession propels everyone into an excited exchange of knowledge and opinions when, after the morning fogs have cleared the bay and the day is hot, the sky a clear dizzying blue, the leaves of the trees not yet summer-dusty, still limp and newborn and moist, the four sit upon the patio lazing, dozing, bathing in the after-death blessings bestowed by the Garretts. The appearance now and then of a hummingbird ethereally suspended above the magenta-throated fuchsia, gives an insubstantiality to unpleasant facts and thoughts. The four appear to bask in a honeymoon, happy to relate their happy dreams — Zita, of her longing for a life of "taste" — a real home with a dining room and a table set with a white cloth, flowers, silver, fine china, with the light and its flowing carefully controlled and distributed.

"Light is everything," she says with vague extravagance. (She is lying on one of the wooden-slatted outdoor sofas arranged on the patio in the shade of the Japanese maple.)

Doris, urged to identify her dream, and unable to compete with those who grasp their dream with such certainty, is silent after murmuring that she can't describe it. And then there is Roger and his desert. Everyone recognizes and perhaps envies that Roger has taken part of the human

162

dream for his own. And how commendable and gentle is Zita's simple longing! And Theo's, to rescue the earth from erosion. The fact that only Roger appears to be prepared to risk death to fulfill his dream, fails to impress in a world where technology is the handmaid of dreamers, where rescuers abound, and the only material problem is the disposal of the dead. The dreams breed admiration. "If only the Garretts were here," they say. "If Irving knew . . . if Trinity could see . . ." It is hard for them to imagine the Garretts dead. They think of them more as vanished travelers in a temporary state of removal. Dying away from home the Garretts therefore wield both the power of their presence, enhanced and rarefied by death, and the power of their absence which holds, like a speck of explosive (that powder which from all appearances may be grains of sugar) the threatened return. The absence keeps a shifting measurement on the scale of death and rarely reaches the point marked by death instead, reaching a total where even death is denied. Or one may describe this as a loss of immunity to absence, when the guests begin saying, "What if the Garretts were to walk in now?"

Then laugh with uneasy guilt, as if they'd be caught stealing—the space used and formerly owned by the Garretts.

"What if they should walk in?"

"They won't."

"What if they do? People have been known to survive burial by earthquake, to be found months after wandering in the hills and valleys, and all the time they were supposedly found, identified and buried . . ."

"And Irving and Trinity knew their way around northern Italy."

"It has been proved they went to the opera. And they were found."

"They have had their memorial service at the retirement home in Carmel. Irving's model city was on display."

"But what if they should walk in here, now?"

This refrain, interwoven with the confessional theme, is repeated daily, usually concluding with Roger's resolution, "Time will tell."

He can make generalities sound undeservedly convincing, his success in this being partly due to his habitual living according to statements where every abstract word begins with a capital letter around which he organizes the governmental architecture of his life. Who can resist that pale sensitive face peering through the archways of the C.'s (Change, Circumstance), the D.'s (Desire, Doubt) the E.'s (Eternity!) the G.'s (Grace, Goodness, Grandeur, Godhead) the T.'s, L.'s and P.'s of Time, Love and Pain?

"Yes," he says, "time is proof enough and will tell what has already been told."

The others are bound to agree.

"People get the life they deserve," Theo says, entering into the rivalry of commonplaces.

"But I doubt if they get the death they deserve." Although Theo also tends to make sweeping statements, he, unlike Roger, is not enclosed and ruled by them and does not feed upon them. Faced with a cliché, Theo is more like the "stout Balboa (or Cortez)" on a hilltop "wildly surmising" and planning possession, for his habit of rescue is not confined to people and includes phrases which in the abundance of his self-confidence he believes to be the result of his exploration in a time-threatened language. He can never see the prints, trails, frozen shadows of all who have been there before him. When Theo and Roger begin this discussion on the "settlements" of people through language, the two women are excluded, stay silent as marked nonentities with not a cliché between them. The men act as if they alone have the right to talk of Life and Death while using their misdemeanors with words to stengthen their destiny- and rescue-obsessed egos.

"I think," Doris begins clearly.

There's no reply. No one is listening.

"As for getting the life one deserves," Zita begins.

No one appears to hear her.

The clichés which the two men use to crown their egos and justify their lives (the dramas of Earth and Desert) are of the same family of commonplaces which make it difficult for the women to "band together."

"Women do not band together as easily as men."

All that women can do together is weep or knit. Zita, an expert in lacemaking, sets up her lace pillow and begins deftly to twist the bobbined thread into her favorite spider-pattern, while Doris talks of her two children, their birth, their first step and word, anecdotes, moments which stay solidly in her mind, becoming mo-nu-ments which take up so much space that they threaten to extend the graveyard of the past into places reserved for the present and future. When the two men begin matching commonplaces, Zita and Doris give up and smile gentle smiles at each other as if to say, "The men" or "the *menfolk*."

Each begins to talk about her husband, not with the intimate sexual detail which French women exchange in railway trains, nor with the stark case notes outlined by New Zealand women in buses and waiting rooms ("His gallstones were the size of boulders"), but nevertheless with a waiting-room tendency to shock and score, and when the waiting is over, Doris goes to Roger, and Zita to Theo, to kiss.

"Two happy couples," they say together, laughing.

"And to think," Roger reminds them," that in a few days I'll be in the desert."

"We'll drive you there," Theo promises, "leave you for a couple of hours and then fetch you."

Roger frowns at the indignity.

"It's serious. It's not a picnic."

"Of course not, but we'll need refreshments afterwards," Zita says.

Doris repeats the word, wonderingly, "refreshments. It's years since I heard or used that word. Ashburton, Ashburton, ten minutes for *Refreshments*. Or was it seven minutes? And if it were lunch it was either *nineteen* or *twenty-three* minutes. Why? *Refreshments*. It's like *fancywork, gocart, wireless, pictures*. Lost."

"I'll take something to eat. And a waterbottle," Roger tells them, sounding hopelessly like a boy who's just seen a film about the desert.

"Even our desert here has to be treated with respect, like the mountains," Theo warns sternly (his record includes two mountain rescues).

"I realize that."

"It will be 130 in the shade."

"I know. I haven't known such temperatures before. This will help to acclimatize me."

"But your skin is so fair, you'll be burned!"

Roger laughs, pleased by Zita's concern.

"Save your sympathy for the *real* journey. Next year maybe."

"But if we do that," Doris protests, "if we value only the *real* journey, what about all those others, journeys and suchlike, that never attain reality? Do we waste our time when they make us weep real tears?"

Theo buys a TV set, twenty-three inch, color, which they can't afford, but Zita, forgetting the new apartment, enjoys the shared feeling of recklessness.

"Have to keep up," Theo says, with the state of constipation and its remedies; deodorants, mouthwash, pet products, bath cleaners, Sky-Blue Sluice and the Blue Fury.

27.

They kept saying, "It's not as if it's the Sahara. It's nothing." They turned their faces toward the sky as if following in imagination the path the warm air had taken from the desert. Oh the beauty of claiming a part of the earth and having others acknowledge the claim!

"This heat will wear us away," Theo said, attuned to the eroding effect of natural forces.

"It will burn our skin."

Zita spoke softly. She was so small, so pretty, and coming from Hungary, an exile for life, she had suffered so much and would never have to prove the fact. "We were refugees . . . ."

And there was comfortable brownbread geranium Doris, a concentration of sympathy except for the intrusion of occasional domestic passions, like on the day when she insisted on finding Parmesan cheese for the evening meal.

"I must, I simply must have Parmesan!"

Roger blushed with embarrassment at her fervor, and when not even the carpeted supermarket had Parmesan and Doris wailed for all to hear, "Nothing but Parmesan will do!", Roger, the spiritual, the desert-dreaming, sank into gloom, and although they survived the meal, the missing Parmesan caused the evening to grow a fungus or blight of its own. They sat watching the Chiller-Diller Movie on Channel Five.

"Perry Mason would be a better choice," Theo said. His build gave him something in common with Perry Mason, he said, and that was one reason he liked to watch him. "And our minds work alike."

The others were too tired to try to demolish or question his certainty.

For the Great Californian Confession was over. There remained only the desert followed by Departure with Trophies. They had even concluded the inevitable episode of "Naked in The Patio," when the heat wave, filling the air with white noise, haze, smog embedded with light, melted all frosty judgment, dissolved middle-age vanities, the glances, the unspoken comparisons, the wild desires, and each person discovered, peacefully, an individual beauty of self, whether a private curve, a softer expanse of skin, an attractive bare-legged stance, an exclusive archway, all of which, shared, gave assurance to the gradually uncaring exposure beneath an unrequiting, wounding sun.

The day before the visit to the desert all went in Theo's car to the supermarket to buy ordinary and "desert" food.

"Will you need salt tablets?" Zita asked.

"Maybe not," Roger answered, trying to keep the journey "polished," untarnished by too many mundane enquiries.

"I'll take a drink and a sandwich."

They waited, trapped in the supermarket while Doris bought an unusual kind of vegetable grater which she knew she couldn't buy in England.

"It's cheap, and weighs only a few ounces," she said, showing it to them. "You put in a battery—the batteries are *worldwide*," (she opened her eyes wide, to suit), "and it does whatever you want it to do—grates, slices, blends, shreds; it makes ringlets, too, and pieces of tomato and cucumber with a hole in the middle."

They listened with pretended or real attentiveness. Roger, again ashamed of her, glanced at the more ethereal

Zita and noted her absorption in the Slow Movement of the Mozart Piano Concerto which the store played from speakers suspended near the deep freeze, the check-out counter and the spy-camera, to relax the customers and entice them to buy more pet food, thousand island dressing, TV dinners, and paper towels.

They came home laden with goods that soon filled the refrigerator, the freezer, the food cupboard and the cupboard beside the dishwasher where the cleaning, polishing, disinfecting, insect-killing supplies were kept.

That night they went to bed early. They made love. Although all except Zita were of an older generation, they could take advantage of the "new" knowledge or acknowledgement and freedom and although they might not easily change persistent habits and preferences or demolish the taboos, say, of oral sex, they did enjoy a happiness their parents had not known. They were sensitive. They cared for each other. The most difficult problem both couples had was that of being honest, admitting occasional failure—not so terrifying if one remembers that sex itself is based on failure—millions of cells that fail beside the few that succeed—and that even in the beginning of life those who do not succeed, in spite of their continued urgency and activity have a reputable, natural destiny!

The next morning they had a breakfast cooked by Doris who "believed in" cooked breakfast. The mood was one of peace. All appeared to be at ease now with the house, its contents, its new owner, the dead Garretts, and one another. Their unspoken fear of a house of the dead had gone leaving them with the strength of householders in charge of their home who yet keep a guest room, seen or unseen, for the death that must come and go, never obtrusive nor obstructing nor advising nor trying to change the routine; always the perfect though ever unannounced guest who did not stay too long, who made it known that he lived elsewhere and in time would return home and send a gracious message of thanks for hospitality shown him, with a reminder—perhaps the hosts might one day care to return the visit, transport provided at his, not their convenience?

At the last minute Zita decided not to go with the others, saying she would spend a quiet morning by herself and be home to welcome everyone after Roger had spent his probationary hour or two in the desert.

28.

They drove through the canyon down into the valley where the air shimmered with heat and already the deer and the snakes were out looking for water. They passed the great mourning redwood trees with the rough bark hanging like strips of dried blood and the tips of the branches, the trusting delicate green of new growth. They passed the valley orchards, the monarch walnut trees, the peach orchards, and then beyond the desolate settlements of mobile homes touched up cosmetically by stands of secluding trees, and the last few road signs, a motel, a stranded take-a-way bar hung with unlit out-of-date Christmas lights, and the sign "Breakfast Juice-Coffee-Two Eggs, Any Style-Hash-99 cents." Then with the goldflanked mountains receding, wavering as if to the throbbing beat of the chemically blue sky, the road gradually became no more than a rough track bordered by desert plants, and ending abruptly beneath the sign DESERT. Already the temperature (read from a huge thermometer attached to the signpost) was 110 degrees.

"I think you're crazy," Theo said, stopping the car. "And it doesn't seem real. In a country like the USA where public information is intimate and discursive, you don't see abrupt signs like that! They'd tell you the area, describe the flora and fauna, and the cost in dollars! See for yourself. Now you know what the desert looks like. Let's turn back before we fry."

171

He spoke as if to an unruly small boy, with a hint of "don't expect me to rescue you."

Roger said nothing. The place did seem like an organized stage setting or the location for a film or a dream, and he too had expected more information, although it could be that for once they were letting the land speak for itself.

He climbed from the car and opening his back pack he drew out a large square of white cloth and draped it over his head, Arab-style, reminding Theo and Doris of the pictures of Lawrence of Arabia. They didn't know where he had found the cloth. It was even possible that he had extracted it from a portrait of Lawrence. He looked slightly mad as he stamped about in his heavy boots (he'd had to give up the dream of going barefoot) with his face peering through the almost enveloping cloth. He wore a long-sleeved cotton jacket and blue and white striped cotton trousers such as spectators wear at tennis or swimming; and some poets, and a few town planners; and this, too, was a denial of his dream of being half-naked. His pack held food and drink for a week, a sleeping bag, a Swiss Army knife for opening bottles and for heroically, swiftly, cutting out the venom of rattlesnakes. The fact that he was planning to spend only an hour or two by himself, quite near where the road ended but far enough to give him the illusion of being alone in the desert, made his elaborately filled pack seem something of a joke.

"Still," he said, explaining, "you never know with the desert." They agreed that you never knew with the desert just as you never knew with the mountains.

Theo, on rescuers' territory, said patronizingly that the heat was a danger in itself if, like Roger, you were not used to it.

"O.K." Roger said. "I'm away."

Sweat was already streaming down his face.

"You have salt tablets?"

That was Doris, seeing a son off the school. You have your coat and hat and handkerchief?

"Don't worry."

At the last minute he had packed a few salt tablets.

"Everything's fine. You'd better go back to the motel. I'll see you in an hour or so. It's a pity I'm not spending the night when the air is cooler and all the creatures are awake." He knew. He had read about it, and seen it on TV.

Doris and Theo were reluctant to leave him. He was already looking quite faint. He shook hands with Theo in a quaint fashion of an explorer, and kissed Doris as if he were leaving her forever, and they watched him plodding along the track, skirting the tangle of chaparral, toward a more even stretch of land that looked like more conventional desert, with cacti, but without the joshua trees, giant saguarros, century plants that his mind already pictured.

When he judged that he was at last away from civilization (he looked back at the car disappearing over the ridge toward the motel) he stopped at the nearest shade, a prickly pear, and sat in its diminished shadow. It was exhaustingly hot. He had soaked his hat in water from the water bottle, but it had dried almost at once in a cloud of steam. He took the bottle and poured water over the cloth and down his face and he could feel it blessing his eyelids and cheeks and trickling down his neck; then he lay with his head pillowed on his pack, and stared up at the molten sky, as he had imagined he would do. He could see what he supposed to be a desert hawk gliding in the air, and he could hear the twitterings of numerous birds. Then he closed his eyes and for the first time, in spite of the heat and the too civilized discomfort (of the kind where, the refrigerator breaking down, and your supply of ice gone, you plunge into your private pool; or, the gas heating having failed, you switch on the electric fire), and in spite of the almost farcical nature of his first visit to the desert, he felt contented, the beginning of his dream realized (and endangered) by its very denial in

173

the satisfaction of the craving for a small taste of reality. He began to feel certain that some vision, some "revelation" would eventually come to him, if not here, for this was merely a rehearsal, but during his "real" journey across one of the great deserts of the world. There was no doubt about this. It was a historical and spiritual commonplace that God always waited in the desert.

A plane droned, glinted, high in the sky. The birds continued their twitterings. There were minute sounds which he could not identify. There was not the imagined silence of the desert, nor among these rocks and pockets of parched soil and cacti scrub were there the oceans of the desert sand that could be whipped to a devil-storm in which, lost, he'd struggle on with the dust in his eyes and hair and face and beneath his eyelids, and he'd stumble and fall, perhaps impaled, as he'd read was the fate of many desert wrens, upon the spines of the cactus or upon a branch of the giant thorn trees that grew without ornament, like stripped selves, or like the trees of the suicides in the Wood of the Second Ring of the Circle of the Violent.

He drowsed. Like a branding iron the heat pressed his body deep into the rock and soil until he might have become a shadow about to disappear, completely controlled by the sun, into the shadowless noon. He opened his eyes. He lay there without any desire to unpack and eat and drink or even soak and splash his face with water. He felt ashamed of being so encumbered with provisions when he knew that the animals and insects and plants of the desert lived from year to year waiting for the few drops of rain which it was their destiny to be given, and which they would receive and store within themselves, never wasting a drop. They received, too, the sand storms and the heat of the "abominable" desert, and fought these powers with their only weapon, their being.

He began to feel irritated with himself for his engrossing concern for the "real" desert, the "real" journey so vivid in his mind, and his reluctance to accept that he was now experiencing a "real" desert. Then he began to feel lonely, and welcomed the feeling. Wasn't it a Sign? He was the frail human being who could never go naked in the desert like the animals, that sweated through their ears and their skin and their tongues, or like the plants, that bore their wallets at their leaf-tips and those that were content with their given nature of blossoming once in twenty years. They were all truly alone. He could never be, not while he needed his pack and his hat and shoes and sunglasses and salt tablets and the car to pick him up when he'd finished his "rehearsal," and his wife in the car and his children in south London with their grandparents and his home in south London with the apple trees and the walled garden, and his friends and even his dead friends, Irving and Trinity Garrett. It seemed to him that his most conspicuous resemblance to a wild animal or plant or insect was the secretion of a kind of glue that also had a power of piercing, or paralyzing or killing, which helped some animals find food and deal with enemies, but which human beings used for recruiting friends and lovers and retaining desired objects, all with a certain confusing intention which resulted in the classification of some friends and lovers and objects as food to be consumed that the host might survive.

He felt tired and lonely and shamefully aware that loneliness was to be pitied, despised, whereas aloneness, set on a higher moral plane, and yet part of the gift of the animals of the desert, was to be admired. Lonely, you are entitled to weep for yourself and your loneliness. Alone, you have the privilege of weeping only for the world beyond yourself, and for the glimpse of God.

The heat grew stronger. The sun seemed to be multiplied, with many suns throbbing down their fire, with the sky like a vast blue foundry furnace, the careless welders having already burned through the ceiling, leaning down, directing their flames to where the mad noon-day Englishman who had not even stolen fire from heaven, lay chained to his desert rock pleading for a vision to fit the pattern of his dream, demanding the reality as well as the dream, his sleeve, at the same time, "singed and not singed" by the "agony of flame."

Open-mouthed, fused with sun, "I do have fortitude," he said suddenly. "Fortitude and God."

He pondered on the word "fortitude," uncommonly in use now, he thought. A word of myth and history and aspiration. His relationship with God was not the kind that is a convenient way of recruiting allies by the assertion, "my life is right, therefore God is on my side." He had thought of the journey to God as a hacking away and removal, first, of dense undergrowth and overgrowth of feeling, particularly of the kind that kept the soul always warm and at ease, although he knew that at the end of the journey the warmth and ease returned. His image of vegetation and bare land, of forest and desert, was one more given cliché that stayed with him. He felt a vague sense of destruction in his inhabiting an image with real flesh and blood.

Ah, but being in the desert now, he was too tired to think anymore, or even to feel. Everything was far away. His head throbbed, suns swirled behind and before his eyes, the shimmer of heat rose and fell upon him in the entranced air that moved like waves on the sea on a day when the air above the water is calm, and in the secret depths of the sea-forest the shadow-flow is in accord with the gentle motion of the "real" sea above, without any sign of that inexplicable fury called a "dry rage" which, beginning in the depths of the sea, in the shadow-territory, can rise to the surface, suddenly thrashing the waves into dark blue and churned foam beneath utterly calm sky and air.

He opened his eyes and stared about him. Controlled again by his image of the "real" desert, he expected to see a mirage of water, the conventional vision of thirsty travelers, a sparkling oasis in a technicolor sunset, the green date palms, the tethered camels resting in the shade. There was no mirage. He saw only a jackhare (he recognized it from the photographs he had seen of the "real" desert). It came to sit by him in the meagre shade of the prickly pear and in Roger's own shade. Roger breathed quietly and kept quite still. The hare was so close, it was quivering all over, panting, its tall ears waving back and forth like cooling fans. It crouched in the small pocket of Roger's and the prickly pear's shade as if unaware of its human company. Roger, in the mood for marveling, despite his discomfort, and realizing that his visit to the desert had so far granted him little advance on his hoped-for vision, felt a joyous gratitude in knowing that the jackhare trusted him enough to seek shade near him, for surely it must be aware of his presence. With the quivering hare crouched beside him, Roger progressed from loneliness to a blessed feeling of shared aloneness. He and the hare were at home together, and this was all that being at home meant, no more, no less. Just sharing a space in peace; not necessarily one that was cottage-size or room-size, or of so many hectares or so many islands and continents, merely a space that was life-size and therefore death-size. Roger and the hare were at home together: they shared a shadow.

The next moment, denying the dream without destroying it, the hare was off with a leap and a bound and a white tail-flash, and out of sight. Roger knew it was time to leave. He picked up his backpack and began to retrace his steps to the edge of the desert and civilization and the sign, DESERT. Then he, in his turn, as a citizen of an apparently literate world, sat in the slight shade offered by the sign and the large thermometer, and waited for Doris and Theo to arrive in the car.

29.

Theo and Doris booked a unit at the Desert Motel.

"We need somewhere to rest, out of the sun for a few hours," Theo explained to the receptionist.

"The sun can be very trying if you're not used to it."

"I'm used to it."

Theo was in an argumentative mood. His head was aching, and he could never bear to be thought a novice in anything, even in being in the company of the sun. One of his repeated descriptions of himself was "a man of experience."

"My accent might be foreign but I'm used to the Californian sun, I've lived here several years, in the Bay area." He spoke the words "Bay area" with the right familiarity and was gratified to note that the receptionist was impressed. He signed the form and took the key.

"There's a coffee bar next door if you want a snack."

She glanced at Doris, thinking, "She's women's Lib and therefore using her maiden name," and accepting that they were oppressed by the heat.

"You have to be careful," she said as Doris turned to follow Theo up the stairs, "He looks really ill."

Upstairs, Theo flung himself on the couch in the sitting room.

"You have the bedroom." he said.

"Don't you want something to eat first? We've brought plenty. It was supposed to be a picnic."

Doris, freed from immersion in the desert sand, to plant a rare, pleasant fantasy, was taken aback at the way Theo, like a small boy in a flower garden chopped off the fantasy's blossoming head with a clean cut. She turned her attention to the food. She wasn't hungry but she had been looking forward to having someone "to herself" without the desert breaking into their life. As for the fantasy, she felt no guilt about that, as Roger had been "saving himself for the desert." All the same, she *was* faithful to Roger. She thought Theo was loud-voiced, opinionated, but she was grateful that he hadn't adopted that special air of having shared secrets which, from her experience, fellow New Zealanders tended to do when one met them in a foreign land, when hometowns as far apart as Napier and Tuatapere, Dargaville and Romahapa were suddenly thought of as neighbors.

"No picnic," Theo said. "I've a splitting headache. I feel quite sick."

He closed his eyes.

Doris went to the bedroom, had a shower and a cool drink and lay on one of the beds. She didn't sleep at once. She thought of her children, and worried about them, that they might be "growing away" from her during her absence: small children were so uncertain about the import of meetings and partings, almost as uncertain as adults but, in their ignorance, with more imaginative scope and more fear. Doris worried about Roger, too, and about the way people kept changing. She had always found change difficult. She remembered how, overnight, her father had changed from a farmer to a commercial traveler, so determined to keep the dignified self he had built as a farmer that he had inadvertently erased it in the clean sweep of becoming a commercial traveler; and she remembered her feeling of betrayal when her mother, once a private person who sometimes wrote verses about Hope and Good Cheer and The

179

Power of a Smile, had become a public landlady whom the boarders addressed as "Mum" when she hadn't been their mother at all. Wellington was a terrible place, Doris thought. She remembered it so vividly like a fairy tale out of her and the world's past—how people had been blown away in the Wellington wind, and when they were found, streets and *gorges* away, there'd be nothing but a heap of dry skin layered like dead leaves, with hair like stalks of grass, and bones ground into white dust that joined the wind in its everlasting cycle of blowing. She had not been homesick for Wellington, unless it was, now and again, for the shady wet side of some of the hill streets where the sun never came, where ferns grew over the fences and between the cracks in the fences and there was a special chill which made you gasp but which you could turn away from at once, though never forget, as if you had been inoculated against perpetual sunlight. Doris was homesick for London. California had a foreigness, a warmth and freedom which she felt to be out of place in her life. It was an intemperate zone while she and her "English" skin had been bred and blossomed in a temperate rain, sun, frost. She felt panic at the harsh way the heat of the California sun and the hot breath from the desert, and the lion-colored mountains rubbed bare by the persistent approaches of dry wind and fire, acted to melt the important inner barriers. She was afraid that she too might change and not recognize herself.

She fell asleep. They had asked the receptionist to phone them in two hours and in almost no time the phone woke her. She went to the sitting room. Theo was still fast asleep. Older men, Doris thought, not remembering where she had heard or taken hold of the idea, older men sleep more. She looked at his slack mouth and heard his heavy breathing. The whole thing, she thought, in a sweeping panic, is out of control. It was strange to think that Theo was from New Zealand, that he knew of the desert places in Central Otago, where the rabbits once had their summer palaces.

Theo had studied them. He knew about them as Lords of Erosion. He knew about the coastline, too, that was slowly sinking into the sea, the cliffs that crumbled away, the tiny new-planted trees that could scarcely hold the devastated soil together (as her cookery book would say, that had no "binding agent") with their fragile roots, while the giant grandfather and grandmother trees lay strewn across the land, or stacked in timber yards "weathering," an insulting attentuation of their hundreds of years of natural weathering; or stood as beams, bargeboards, weatherboards in thousands of homes, each night cracking and sighing and groaning, nerve-twitching at the scars of the old amputations; at night, when the hedgehog was snuffling along the path, and the morepork was calling.

The thought that Theo knew about such things made her feel more kindly towards him. She touched him gently on the shoulder. She thought he looked older than sixty-five whereas during the day, awake, he never failed to give the impression of nimble youth.

Slowly he opened his eyes. He looked dazed.

"I've a frightful headache," he said. "The heat."

He frowned.

"I don't think I can see clearly."

His voice slurred slightly.

"I . . . the words have gone . . . I can't think of the words . . . what's happened? My right arm is strange . . . heavy . . . My God!" Doris felt distaste and fear. For a moment, Theo, the powerful all-rescuing Theo, looked like an old scarecrow, just clothes and imitation face and body and empty sleeves. A shabbiness that made him appear so, cast its career-mark upon his no-face as surely as any profession may mark the skin with its identifying sign — the calm doctor with the indoor, centrally-heated skin, the smooth salesman with the leather-suitcase look, the eye forever persuading and guaranteeing.

"What is it, Theo?" Doris asked.

"I think . . . a slight . . . stroke."

"Shall I phone a doctor?"

"There's really no . . . yes perhaps—does my voice sound pec . . . funny . . . the words seem to have been removed."

Doris persuaded him to stay on the couch while she phoned for a doctor.

Dr. Quarles, from the Sun Valley Estate (Retirement, Privacy, Organized Leisure, Medical Care, Shopping Mall), was a small man of middle age. When he heard Doris speak he exclaimed, "You're English! You will know the poet Francis Quarles?"

"No," Doris said. "I may have heard of him, but I don't go in for poetry. I do seem to remember the name from school days."

"You don't know Francis Quarles, chronologer of the City of London, several centuries ago? You don't know, 'Disclose Thy Sunbeams, Close Thy Wings and Stay' — that's from 'Wherefore Hidest' . . . ?"

"I'm afraid I don't," Doris said abruptly. "Here's your patient."

"He's an ancestor," Dr. Quarles explained. "We had our tree done."

"But this is *my* field," he said, seeing Theo, "yes my field," as if staking a territorial claim in an area blossoming not with words but with strokes and heart attacks, with a mine of auxiliary riches (medical aids, wheelchairs, and so on) yet to be exploited.

"I'm into geriatrics. I'm used to these vascular accidents."

"Vascular accidents?" Doris said, wonderingly.

"Yes. Can you get him home to rest?"

"We're leaving for home in a few minutes," Doris said.

"Your husband will have to take things easily. And see his own doctor. These accidents have to be watched."

"An accident?"

"No strain, no anxiety. A check-up with his own doctor."

It was unusual for Theo to be silent; he had transferred much of his speech to his eyes and his left hand. Doris found that in speaking to him she was now raising her voice as if he were deaf. She realized, too, that he was no longer trying to speak, as if his few words had been a surge of his power of speech before the extinguishing of it.

"Will it come back?" she asked him.

He nodded. He could have meant yes or no.

Dr. Quarles was just as indefinite, "Time will tell."

It was decided that Doris should drive to fetch Roger while Theo rested at the motel with the receptionist looking now and again, for a fee, of course, in the country of the curled hand.

And when Doris and Dr. Quarles had gone, Theo lay on the couch remembering the doctor's words, "It's a warning. From now on . . . ." and finishing and imposing many more sentences. Theo was glad that Zita had stayed home. They'd so often talked and teased each other with his advancing age ("Remember you're going to look after me when I'm a helpless old man"—spoken with laughter and a flexing of muscles, gymnast-style) that the idea had become so much the reality that there was no room for the other reality, the terrible rather than the harmless replica created out of the denials constantly made by Theo's fine figure, his youthful energy, his philosopher-shock of white hair (somehow protective), his clothes which Zita chose, carefully matching youthful patterns and colors, buying only the "best" which often meant the costliest: handmade shoes, silk pajamas. Why, there was no room for disablement in that dream! Theo Carlton and his beautiful young wife. People looked at them admiringly wherever they went. He and Zita had come a long way from frozen narrow-minded New Zealand which, if the deer and the opossums and the bulldozers did not first consume it, was slowly sinking into the sea anyway, its earth sliced off as if the land were no better than a round of stale bacon or a diseased limb. Or a great dead fish going back to the sea where it belonged. Yes, they had come a long way from New Zealand!

To this. To Stroke Country, and the slicing away of his own power and youthfulness and a scattering of all his words with some falling out of reach, whittled away, like that time years ago when his father was tallying the shop receipts, all the supplies carefully paid for, and a wind came through the open window and carried them out along the street and up in the air. . . .

Zita would nurse him. Frightened, sympathetic, she would nurse him in his increasing frailty, the nurse gradually replacing the wife, in a reality that, in spite of their laughing acceptance, they had never wanted to be. Ever. This was only the beginning. Dr. Quarles had said it was not as serious as it might appear, at his age. No residue, though that must be checked, only a weak right arm and a more prolonged searching for words. A Warning only. Theo thought of all the other realities lying in wait. He thought of the Garretts stacking up their beautiful replicas, their marble table, their wooden Shakespeare — how Zita and the Prestwicks had talked about it one night in the sitting room —even about the replicas of time in those curious photos of the Garretts at different ages, and, funnily enough, Zita had been sitting there sewing a *transfer*, an historic scene which she had traced on to the linen, then crumpled the tissue paper where the original print of the original scene had been marked, and choosing her own colors and her desired thickness of thread she had begun to make the scene her own. The others admired it, too. He seemed to remember that it was a scene from a battle, realistic, with blood too. The Battle of — Hohenlinden, Heavenfield, Blenheim, Maldon . . . ?

30.

Roger waited beneath the road sign. The heat still swirled about him, breaking its waves over him and seeming to flow on, bearing away the top of his head in a burning slice. He felt at once transparent, insubstantial, dispersed, and broken by the heat. He wanted to sob. The sun was the word made world in the midst of the golden landscape where grass was steel, and thin and aged, growing beside the young punchgrass hit relentlessly by the champion sunwind, yet springing back to attention; a world where small soft-feathered crimson birds impaled themselves upon the thorns.

In the confusion of sun and its heat Roger felt, ashamed, a premonition of failure. Today's visit to the desert was a rehearsal only, and if this was the effect of the heat, how could he stay sane on a "real" journey? Or had he learned more from this journey and there'd be no need to test the reality of the dream? Why should he? It was in trying to test the reality that one met all the problems and failures, not only of the thing itself but of the mind that is occupied obsessively with dualism. In the moment of closeness with the jackhare, Roger came to believe that not only was his life a gift to himself and to others, but his share of light from the sun, and the shadow the sun created from his shape were also at once his property and his gift to others. Why indeed go to a "real", "utter" desert? Even the mechanics of driving the few miles from the Garretts house had been unnecessary. He knew that he was not trapped into surviving by the currency of the acceptably real. Yet why persist for a closer and closer share until one became burned like a transfer upon the vast original embroidery?

There was still no sign of the car with Doris and Theo. Looking down at his skin Roger felt that the beads of sweat trickling down were blobs of melting flesh, that he was beginning to melt, like wax, and even if he had wings like Icarus, they too would melt: wings were not guaranteed to be permanent. He had seen the replica in the Kensington Museum of the man who constructed his wings from feathers: even without trying to fly, suspended in the museum, the birdman's wings, consumed by moths, had not escaped attack.

Roger closed his throbbing eyes. He could faint, he thought, and no one would know. He had become part of the peculiar hierarchy of hare, man, road sign. He could die here, in this narrow literate shadow before he could fulfill his dream; he could die known as a man
"whose work had
come to nothing
Bred to a harder thing
than Triumph . . .
be secret and exult,
Because of all things known
that is most difficult."

Still no sign of the car. No animals, not even the jackhare, which having made its alarming mistake of seeking the shade of a man, as if men were trees, had disappeared forever; only the sound of birds twittering, chuckling, warbling from hidden places.

Then Roger saw the car, flashing like a skyrocket, like a car-shaped sun traveling, glitteringly polished, blazing light with its mirror-power casually catching the sun in a bonfire of steel and chrome. The car looked so rich, jewel-like in its

186

advance, as if being a carrier and killer of mere people and goods were a debasement of its use. He could see that Doris was driving, no doubt chromium-suited and shod, bearing mirrors on her breasts to cast fire whenever they flashed in the path of the sun.

"She shouldn't be driving," Roger said, a sudden outcast from sun-plane and desert-dream. "She's not a good driver." And why was she alone in the car?

Doris stopped the car and opened the door.

"For heavens sake come out of this heat!"

Nobly, without speaking, Roger heaved his pack into the car and climbed in beside Doris.

"I'm driving," she said.

He glanced at her. Nothing, he thought, could remove that healthy bloom from her cheeks. Yet, she too looked overcome by the heat and her blue eyes were darker than usual, like a sky adjusting to the presence of another sky, refusing to submit in brilliance, as colors do; at war, and returning splendor for splendor. She looked afraid. How like her, Roger thought, to be so concerned for me! He felt a surge of love toward her, and she, absorbent as moss, received it as if it were rain. But why did she appear so frightened? He was safe, wasn't he?

"It's over now," he said, reassuring her. "The heat is terrible."

She answered with unexpected briskness.

"Theo's been taken ill. A mild stroke. He's O.K., but we should hurry home."

"Mild stroke! It affects the brain!" Roger said, shuddering at the awful power of the word "brain" which in some aspects of life had replaced the word "God" in evoking awe. The brain, the heart, the lungs. Their deadly power and those who appointed themselves guardian of it were always in the news.

"People have such attacks every day," Doris said, "and get up and walk away." She had heard that said of someone struck by lightning, but she spoke as if it were comparable to being shot or hit by a car or knocked out by an opponent in a fair fight. Roger listened, impressed once again by her practicality, which had developed strength as his preoccupation with dreams and ideals increased. This was the Doris who could arrange the household, look after the children, search relentlessly for Parmesan cheese, while her husband searched for God. There was a time when she would set aside her domestic affairs to read books aloud with him, listen to music, enjoy the heavenly organization of a Bach fugue, but as the children were born she had so little time to share his world, and his sharing of the duties of the household, instead of giving her more time, appeared to make her more preoccupied with domestic concerns while increasing his own distaste for them.

"I'm a homemaker," Doris would say proudly. Her rosiness and softness had great appeal for Roger's friends, and those who were gay, lonely for family, used their special maternal talents to give the children a wealth of love and care. Roger remembered how someone had even asked Doris the name of her perfume, "Isn't it some kind of flower?" he asked, before he realized with embarrassment that it was the smell of her skin, of her self and her life naturally in blossom.

"Poor Theo," Doris said, seizing the dominant reality, as usual, and paying no attention to Roger's experience in the desert, not even to ask how it had been. He felt disappointed, and slightly jealous of Theo, who, after all, had his loving wife to give him sympathy. He knew they had all been worried about the visit to the desert, and they'd talked of little else for days. They would want to know the outcome, surely. Some time, they would want to know. He had felt that in the past few days Doris had begun to understand and share his dream, and his need for it. He therefore felt the news of Theo's illness to be like a personal robbery. He felt that if suffering were in the air, like rain, it should fall on him if only so that he could explain the pattern of its falling, tell about it like a tourist reporter, deliver to himself a luxury of guilt which he could live on for the rest of his life. The guilt was a new aspect. If it hadn't been for his obsession with the desert . . .

He waited for Doris to censure him.

If it hadn't been for your wanting to go to the desert this might never have happened to Theo . . .

She said only: "We must get Theo home at once. Out of this heat."

The motel came in sight. They parked the car and went to the room where they found Theo waiting, looking newly frail but too apprehensive to draw attention to it and unable, in the drought of words, to make his usual jocular assertion of being "in perfect health."

"Sorry," he said. "It's slowed me down. All this."

He waved his left hand vaguely as if the "vascular accident" were part of the surroundings, rented with the motel room. They saw that when he moved he limped slightly.

"Hadn't we better eat before we go?" Doris asked.

"There's food in my pack." Roger said at once. "I didn't touch it, only the water. You see, when —"

His visit to the desert was being passed over without even casual mention, as if he'd returned from shopping, strolling along a civilized street.

"Do you feel well enough for traveling?" he asked Theo.

Theo nodded. Then with an effort he said, "I may have to stop all close . . . work."

"Your eyes?"

"No close work."

As far as they knew, reading, microscopic examination of soils, and the writing of his book were Theo's "close work," and apart from these he was a "panoramic" man, a stout Balboa or Cortez, whether you subscribe to poet or historian; yet by the way he said it he seemed to be including in his past habitual "close work" numerous activities such as embroidery, lace making, watch making, picture restoration, bacteria cultivation; and thus, by his manner, he gave the image of a man with a vastly restricted future. No more close work! Roger could see the sympathy in Doris's eyes, and on her lips, their very slight movement and moistness.

They agreed to have something to eat, after which they set out for the Garretts' place, on a formal journey where they deliberately ignored the present and ceremoniously returned life and ownership of the home to Trinity and Irving Garrett.

"Not long now, to the Garretts'," Roger said.

He was feeling shocked, dismayed, irritated by what had happened. It was so out-of-place in the midst of his newly acquired experience of the desert. (Roger was an experiential snob—a search for God made him a better person than Doris in her search for Parmesan cheese, even if her search was chiefly to feed him and prolong his life so that he could continue his own search.) He did not feel that Theo's "accident" belonged in the same "class" as his own time in the desert or as the injury or illness he might suffer in his journey to the "real" desert. To be taken ill in a motel! In a human parking lot! He felt that he might not now be able to tell them of his experience (which in his mind was gaining importance and a touch of the divine), of the hare that chose to shelter in his shadow. It did not seem undignified that for a few moments his own shadow had been used as a parking lot!

31.

Alone in the Garretts' house, Zita enjoyed the vividly experienced absence of Theo, Roger, and Doris. She thought of Roger in the desert and she heard in her mind his "Oxford accent" talking, talking of his "real" expedition. He always sounded superior to the others. This classification by voice fascinated her, sometimes made her afraid, as if accent were a matter of life and death, and she understood why her mother never had the courage to learn English, although New Zealand English, as an offspring of "standard" English allied to other varieties and Polynesian intonation, had a pleasant neutrality as if it had been suitably "fixed" or "altered" like a cat in danger of breeding a colony of cats. Roger's voice was the New Zealand elocutionary voice, like that of the schoolmaster or some of the radio announcers who'd been "taught." "Three tired toads trying to trot to Tilbury Towers," etc. But it was so unlike what Zita supposed was the "real" Roger that she pitied him for being the victim of yet one more deceit of language, especially harmful in that it was practiced as soon as Roger spoke, and tended to inspire resentment and ridicule from those who, uncomfortably aware of past imperial domination, rebelled as a matter of course against the "marble-in-mouth" accent of some Englishmen. Yet everyone listened when Roger spoke. The harsh clarity of his tone was electric, every consonant and vowel uttered exactly as if they were part of the usual speech training exercises:

The silk-suited superfluous suitors were suitably attired in the pursuit of Sue who will soon superintend the choosing and the ensuing furiously suicidal salute of the superfluous suitors.
Or:
Gold flattery is old fiction, feigned, felicitous, a gold favorable feature in a familiar mould.

Zita was proud to have learned English. It lay richly plaited within her native language and her vocabulary of many words in other languages. She was convinced that, whereas those for whom it was a native tongue were forever being tangled in it, impaled upon it, she would never be harmed by it. She felt that she wore an armor, like the clothing that Roger had told her about, worn by the desert travelers in America to protect them from the thorny chaparral. Roger had studied so much about the desert, from quantities of books and photographs and only a few days ago had persuaded them to sit for two hours watching a documentary on the color television, desert scenes and inhabitants with advertisements directed at the vast number of unwashed, unshampooed, stinking, pimpled, constipated Americans living in dust-ridden houses, sleeping between dirty grey sheets in a world of cockroaches, ants, fleas and the Common Cold.

"You have to ignore the advertisements," Roger had said, coughing in response to the white-coated actor testing the latest cough cure. Zita had thought he looked very poetic when he coughed. Such fair skin, such a sensitive appearance of frailty. Theo had said to her, sneeringly, that Roger looked to be the "English type" who couldn't bear to be in a draft for fear of catching a cold, and so how could he survive the great wide heat-draft of the desert?

In his absence, then, Roger left the sound of his voice, a memory of the colors he chose to wear—dull greens, greys, yellows, and his unexpectedly fervent praise of Zita's lace making.

The absence of Theo brought peace as well as a feeling of loneliness. *His* presence was in his bulk, his tall manly

192

figure, his shock of curly hair, his vitality which, consuming that of others, left him with an extra supply. His words were spoken at a pitch which gave them a rolling friction like the sound of a concrete mixer several meters away or, more kindly perhaps, the turning and turning of river-pebbles being polished in a tumbler, to come out as precious stones; or maybe the rotating of the marbles being used to decide the winner of a national lottery; whatever the comparison, his voice carried further than Roger's arrow-sharp tone. Theo's continued loud cataloguing of his rescues always made Zita nervous, particularly if Theo had been drinking his favorite wine, for then his voice became louder, his rescues more numerous and detailed, the indebtedness of the world to his actions greater, the public recognition more longed-for, and the love for Zita and the perfection of their marriage more volubly stressed, all of which meant that when the evening was over and they were in bed, Theo, the sensitive, thoughtful husband had been replaced by the loud-voiced, violent rescuer crying out for recognition and satisfaction. Yet it was the wild, drunken Theo, loud in his profession of love and care for Zita, which seemed to strengthen her love for him, for when Theo was in such a mood she disliked him so much and felt so repulsed by his bullying of her and others, that they were both so "undone" by each other that in their loving, their selves (broken to pieces like two priceless vases flung from their accustomed place where they stood day after day receiving light together, shadowed in unison in equivalent corners and curves, seeing the same view, surrounded by the same furniture) became as if attended by a good angel who, picking up the pieces, gently reassembled them without a seam or sign that they had been broken. Zita's fear was that some day or night the healing angel, who gave this reality to their dream of love, would fail to attend them, leaving them face to face with the deplorable unrealities of an imitation life and love.

Thinking about Theo, she felt more lonely for him, as a

193

prisoner might be lonely for her captor, for she knew herself to be his prisoner, (although she often rebelled against being so) she was aware that he avoided leaving her to go out alone, and, in company, stayed constantly by her side. During her marriage she had not once walked along the street alone: both she and Theo boasted about this; nor had she shopped alone nor visited friends. This was his choice, his command, his definition of their marriage. She found it not too unpleasant to be possessed like a human doll, to be given whatever clothes and jewels she desired; and then to be put on display by Theo as "my lovely young wife, my Zita." My Zita, my toy, my doll, my princess, my wife. She was the female spider in the tower making lace from corner to corner of her world.

A practical problem, however, in being decked with real diamonds and pearls, was that the prince was a retired lecturer on a pension, with little money and little sense of it, and therefore constantly in debt. When the bills came, Zita would read them and put them aside with the magical conviction that simply by handling them and studying them she had in some way paid them. She knew that Theo performed a similar sleight of reality, fitting his philosophy of recklessness with money to his manipulation of circumstance; they both constantly found a new excuse for not being able to afford a home of their own, Theo's latest being his ancestry, how, all his forebears having lived to "a great age during which all good fortune came to them," there was plenty of time still to get the home they had always wanted.

"After all," he said, "one of my ancestors was a schoolfellow of Lord Byron."

In some way this fact also helped to explain the recklessness with money.

Zita had observed that, preoccupied with his rescues, Theo was often strangely insensitive to the complex feelings of the rescued, and, when she heard him repeating the story of how he had rescued her, she felt her gratitude being eroded by the repetition, while her love, embedded in that

194

gratitude, became worn, changing in shape and texture, and promising or threatening to become unrecongizable, yet remaining, like a crushed shell within a rock, inevitably fitting whatever surrounded it.

Ah Theo, the conqueror, the reckless spender, the beloved guest in most households, the inspired lecturer always ready with the exciting, balancing *Why not?* in triumph over the agonizingly eternal *Why*. Theo, for whom time was an ally rather than an enemy. Theo, who bound himself to the rescued by keeping in "touch" with each one. For one who could so question the order of the events, he showed unusual faith in the idea that life was a journey and the longer you had been on the journey the nearer you were to your destination and the fulfillment of all your dreams; that living was like any trail or elephant walk or flat race in a straight line. Yet he had made his life's work the study of erosion — say, the erosion of a mountain that submitted only to time and weather, never journeying in the sense of going somewhere, yet slowly stripped layer by layer of its existence and identity. Zita knew that Theo's interest in erosion was not merely academic, and she was grateful for this, particularly since they had been living in California where she had met armies of town planners, engineers, geologists, botanists who may have done field work at some time but who appeared to be interested only in theorizing and writing papers on their subject. Year after year, they wrote and published their papers, spurting out, every two or three years, like a kind of overflow from an injection of anaesthetic, the required bibliography for circulation within the universities. Zita had been naïve enough to want to know which towns Irving had planned. She had been astonished when he said, "Oh, I've not planned any *real* towns. I can't drive you to one of my towns. They're not built. My plans are studies, exercises. It's one of the facts of academic life. I do have my model town, though. My dream city."

How satisfied he must have been, Zita thought, when he

learned he had been chosen by Blenheim, New Zealand, Berkeley's twin city, as the visiting expert in town planning! He had told her how, early in his career, he imagined that one day he would take his friends to a hilltop and point to a panorama of a cluster of buildings set harmoniously within a desirable landscape, and say, "That's *my* town." But as his career advanced he learned it was simpler and more profitable for him to write a book that occupied a tabletop than to hope that his realized dreams would spread over hundreds of acres of land. Whatever Blenheim might have been, then, it was, in a sense, to have become Irving's heaven.

Alone, thinking of the other guests, and slowly coming to accept Theo's absence, Zita began to enjoy her feeling of freedom. She walked from room to room in the Garretts' house, as if it were her own home. She wondered why the Garretts had left everything to someone they didn't even know. That woman writer who stayed downstairs out of sight in the studio apartment, who said she was deciding what to "do" with the place, and who had—oh, generously —asked them to choose their keepsake of the Garretts— what claim had she to the house and its contents? She said she was writing a book, and you had to believe her, because she had written two books already, but these days everyone was writing a book, and there was no need to have the disaster or the unique experience before you wrote the book; in fact you could start with the film and then write the book and then have the disaster or the unique experience. And what had Alice Thumb written that had persuaded the Garretts to leave her their *entire estate*? It was a will made at the last minute, too, when they'd only just met the woman. Perhaps it was because she said she had lived in Blenheim, the twin city, and she would have been able to tell Irving about it, and suggest what improvements he might make, as a visiting expert.

Zita went to the kitchen and rejoiced in being alone there. No Doris, the solid practical person, rather like a

196

female version of Theo without his rescue mania. A potential rival, perhaps; and yet, though intelligent, with a useful knowledge of geography, though flourishing in domesticity, and a good if unimaginative cook, Doris was hardly the princess type which Theo needed and had found. Doris was tenacious in command of her household, no doubt; she was, also, too wholesome; no one, Zita thought, would ever make her the subject of rumor or the object of persecution.

Zita felt that it was years since she had a chance to think her own thoughts instead of the shadow thoughts of Theo. He was so powerful, and she was so absorbed in his life that she hadn't had time to take a separate path of thought, and if she had tried, it had always been a short dead-end route that forced her return to the original highway. And then she was so busy enjoying her life and her clothes, designing and sewing many of them; cooking imaginative meals, decorating and redecorating the downtown apartment; and making her lace with the lace pillow she'd had for so long now that it was worn threadbare in its gold velvet. Yes, Theo had indeed rescued her. If it hadn't been for him she might now be going from unhappy love affair to unhappy love affair or living miserably on her brother's Southland farm, or teaching in Invercargill and watching students she had known at training college get that grey anxious look, fearful of damage among the quicksilver children. As for Invercargill—oh that grey city nearly at the southern most part of the world, where the wind direct from Antarctica blew, rain-and snow-laden, from end to end of the wide, grey streets!

In some ways, Zita thought, her and Theo's brands of madness were suited. She remembered the night when, having had too much wine, he began throwing kerosene on the barbecue fire, changing it to a leaping bonfire which threatened the apartment building. She'd not stood by pleading, "Don't, Theo, you'll set fire to the apartment" as she knew Doris would have done. Doris would have taken control and drawn Theo away, treating him like a naughty

197

child. No, Zita, who was both the child and the princess, had snatched at the kerosene and joined Theo in feeding the fire, shouting crazily at it, daring it to burn them and the building and the city and the world, for what did they care? They stopped only because they had no more kerosene and no more rage, and they'd opened another bottle of wine, talking drunkenly to each other, and that night she'd been able to bear his love making and had fallen asleep in his arms listening to his whimpering and sobbing like a heartbroken child whose toy wouldn't wind anymore. In many ways he too was still a child. He quickly felt rejected—by his friends when they tired of his arrogance and boasting, and by his country which, he felt, never gave him the recognition he deserved for his pioneer work on Erosion, and this when half the people in the top positions in foreign affairs, internal affairs, agriculture and fisheries, had been put there by him—a word from him a letter, a rescue or two, and there they were at the top, some with knighthoods; and schools named after them . . . .

He was a disappointed child, the little prince with his princess; and, childless by her own choice, Zita knew she would always care for him and rock him to sleep and when he was old and sick she would comfort him. Her thoughts always returned to this. It was an anchoring place for both her and Theo, and there was a shared pain in thinking of it which gave them real pleasure. It was all planned, as clearly as Irving Garrett's paper and cardboard towns, and Roger's expedition in the desert, and Doris's household management and her new hobby of varnishing and preserving maps of countries of the world; and Zita's own patterns of lace and embroidery. It was a wonderful dream, their being together. They were a perfectly matched couple.

Zita, her thoughts home again, prepared a cold meal for the others and went to the patio to eat her sandwich lunch. The new-leaved tree growing tall at the edge of the garden spread its green-tinted light over her. This house could be ours, she thought. No more rented apartments. We could be living here. That woman writer doesn't need the house: Alice Thumb, Violet Pansy Proudlock, Mavis Halleton, whatever she calls herself. She's a stranger, and although we were not very close to the Garretts, we had our shared interests. They were not the kind of people anyone knows well; they had a neutrality, a pallor, a smoothness of feeling that gave others so little grasp of them. And they had no family, and no relatives living.

We would redecorate of course, Zita said to herself. That mask of Shakespeare with the burn holes in his forehead— we'd get rid of that. Roger and Doris might like it for an English keepsake. And Theo will have the study with that wall chart of the condensed history of mankind (we'll keep that, though I'm sure Doris has her eye on it), and we'll (she had subtly shifted tenses) be at home for the first time in our married lives. And some days we'll go out into the High Sierras and the desert (Roger's obsession with the desert has made us feel that it belongs to him). And in the evenings we'll have dinner parties with my lace tablecloth on the table, and the flowers we have grown, and we'll sit and talk and Theo will be brilliant and witty, with just one or two rescues recounted, and explained, and the top people in the top positions named
his rescue his influence
the people in top positions
spinning spinning only by his courage and perception
"I knew what to do. I recognized his gift . . ."
"He was wasting his life . . . A word from me . . . I put him in touch with . . . I moved my knight and so he was able to advance his rook while the bishop, momentarily free . . ."

The day was quiet with only the sound of distant traffic, an occasional train whistle, near bird song from the many birds, which Zita could not name and did not try to, for though she had a tenderness for all living creatures she had no desire to learn the personal names of birds and trees and thus be bound to them and responsive, against her will, to their demands. She was happy to have the trees shade her and the birds sing to her. As for the flowers she loved, she knew only a few of their names, restricting the family and preserving herself from the worry over their frailty. To her they were all flowers to display in the garden in their earth-bed or in the house, in vases, cut without the cry of "poor things it's cruel to pick them." She picked them and burned the ends of their stems (like burning the soles of their feet, someone said to her in horror) to make them last, for flowers were no use dead. In her learning of English she had never reached the stage of poetic rejoicing in names, almost as if, had she gone beyond the learning of essential names, she might have been taken over by the English language as surely as the nations in the Wall Chart of the Condensed History of the World had been conquered and their tiny column of red or grey or blue or green erased. This was one area where she clung to her Hungarian nationality; a small column within her that would not be erased.

(The wall chart read thus:

"This chart graphically represents the progress of man from the dawn of civilization to the present. Each nation or ethnic group is shown by a color band with dates of important events and persons to the right. Reading downward one may follow the rise and fall of empires, the emergence of new cultures and the migration of others. With a glance across the chart the reader can view developments in all parts of the world at a particular moment in history. The relative expansion and decline of world powers is indicated by the width of the columns. Stripes of a different color show conquest or strong influence by an outside nation. When a nation loses its political or cultural identity the column merges into that of the conquering group.")

Zita had noticed that Doris was interested in the names of things and Theo approved of her many questions — "see that plant there, the one with the pointed leaves and the red streak, what is it?" Both Theo and Roger liked to know names, with Roger's questions beginning with "why" and Theo's with "how." Zita realized that she was a *Where* person. She could never explain (in an age of explanation it was necessary) the delight she felt in "placing" objects where she felt they would be most at home. She would stand seemingly for hours before a piece of furniture trying to decide where to set it to its own (and not her) advantage. She was forever arranging and rearranging, not in a state of restlessness as some women move furniture because they cannot bear the sameness of an exterior view that could be interior, but because she genuinely desired to see "everything in its place," not as an alphabetical catalogue or some superior "system" but in its place of beauty where the light could fall on it, creating patterns of shade; or in an arrangement of curtains, the window being denied light and a darkscape formed there, while all the other windows filled to the flamebrim with a shimmering swelling wave in a liquid grey-green light that poured into the room. Here, in the Garretts' house it would be the three redwood trees, their branches brushing the wall, propping up their brighter new growth, and the smoky grey fog flowing up from the Bay which, instead of the known southern sun, colored the light-wave.

Zita knew a sense of power in her domestic arranging. She felt she could truly be herself with her armies of tables, chairs, sofas, beds, ornaments, the carpet battlefield assuring her control of the invasion of the sun and moon into the space occupied by her and Theo, and her choosing with her lace and crochet and embroidery the color of the banners they would wave from their windows to call for help or signal victory.

How pleasant it was on the patio! Surely the heatwave was breaking? Lying under the unnamed tree, Zita knew the luxury of being arranged rather than arranging, as if the sun and its leaf-light had placed her there. She closed her eyes and drowsed and the image of Josef's farm came to her, of the bright green paddocks waterlogged after rain, and the earth churned to a stinking bog by the traffic of the cows to and from the milking shed; that would be how it was now, in June. She remembered the old cowbyre, its roof the sky, with the roughly made wooden bail and its iron pegs and the trough in front for the house-cow to chew her winter hay or turnips, the cow's broad yellow flat teeth like rows of worn ivory logs. Southland. Everyone said it was turnip country —swedes, mangolds—everywhere with their floppy leaves and their spinning-top-shaped bodies banded with dull red and creamy yellow and their flesh pale gold, full of sweet juice; and the cut pieces of turnip, like shapes out of geometry, forming natural pyramids and cylinders: a sweet geometry, for they used to eat the shapes sprinkled with sugar.

She could remember turnips in Hungary, too. Like Southland, it was turnip country. When people asked her would she ever return there she always answered, "perhaps some day." But she knew she would be afraid. She remembered the way the soldiers formed in the streets in a webbed pattern that prevented escape, and how she had seen the escaping people shot, where only a year before, within the same pattern, there had been cheering, flags waving, the band playing, when the army marched along the street.

Theo was a good man. She would never give up Theo. He had rescued her. She would cling to him now, and even when he died, she would stay close to him, she would be like that blue flower—what did Doris say was its name?— only yesterday they talked of it—ah, *morning glory*, clinging to the bark of the tree that gave it support although the tree itself was dead, leafless, headless, without branches.

Zita woke suddenly from her drowsing. She heard the car being driven into the carport. Roger was home from the desert.

"Theo!"

202

She felt as if her life had been suspended and was only now beginning again.

"Theo!"

Abruptly disarranging herself from the pattern in the sun-frame she ran out to meet him, brushing by the morning glory that grew by the path and glancing at it as at a stranger. As for the dead tree which it embraced, she ignored it, and ran to the car.

32.

"He has been taken ill," Doris warns as Zita approaches the car. "It must have been brought on by the heat."

"We told him he shouldn't go to the desert. Or we thought it. I don't think he's very strong, he's an indoor man, he's English; the heat of the desert . . ."

Zita stops, bewildered, as she sees Roger apparently in good health, opening the back door of the car. He calls out to her, "He should go to bed at once, to rest."

Zita frowns. "Was Theo in the desert too?"

"No, he was taken ill at the motel."

Zita gasps, quickly drawing in breath. "It's Theo then? What happened?"

But surely it's alright, there is Theo climbing out of the car and waving to her and coming toward her. He is paler than usual and he speaks slowly with gaps between words, but they are only gaps, not steep, isolated chasms.

"A . . . dizzy . . . turn. It's O.K. darling."

"The sun. In this heat wave. Even those used to the sun as you are, Theo . . ."

He clearly wants to say "yes, it was the sun," because once he admits weakness, disease, he feels that he might lose his life's parcel of prestige and confidence. He and Zita have sworn to be honest with each other—that is easy enough, he feels, but how can he be honest with himself?

He agrees. "Yes, the sun. Sunstroke. It's common."

Hearing him, Doris and Roger look surprised, then relieved that the game of explanations has been simplified. Yet they observe the transparent fear in Zita's face as the dreaded thoughts overtake her: something has happened to Theo. He is suddenly, with the intervention of the truth, no longer the "old" Theo. Her fear is stronger for her knowing that Theo's hopes like medals awarded to himself are *pinned* on his retaining a power that can make void the guarantee of physical and mental change, the only guarantee which, they know in their hearts, has never been known to fail; and yet because she believes in Theo she has also believed in his denial of the guarantee. She wishes now that his illness were serious enough to force them both to realize that their changelessness was a dream and that change need not be a continued nightmare. She reveals none of these thoughts. She laughs.

"Sunstroke! Theo, you naughty boy. I'm surprised at you."

"He must rest," Doris insists in a neutral-sounding tone, not hysterical with advice which must be taken or else, yet not without a sensible concern. She has been jealous of everyone's desire to protect Zita and of her evident willingness to be protected, her magnetic vulnerability, while Doris feels herself to be as ordinary and unspectacular as a lawn handkerchief—useful, clean, capable of attending to tears and then being folded, square and concealed.

"The doctor at the motel says he must rest," Roger says.

Both Doris and Roger wait for Theo to tell the truth, to complete the circle of information, smoothly, instead of leaving a jagged triangle capable of wounding, even of drawing blood—whose?

Having established that Theo has simply "been a naughty boy," Zita takes charge.

"I'll put him to bed at once and you call the doctor—Dr. Grant down on Oak Street. The number's in the phone book. Come dear, lean on me."

Any other time, "lean on me" would rouse laughter. Big burly Theo. Frail golden-haired Zita, lace-woven. Lean on me!

She helps Theo into Irving Garrett's study which is their bedroom, the Prestwicks, having flown in from "else-where" having been granted the "master" bedroom. As she turns back the sheet of the double foldaway bed beneath the Chart of the Condensed History of Civilization, she recalls her fantasy of owning the house, this room being Theo's study, his desk there in the corner by the window, the foldaway bed made up as a daybed, and their bedroom the "master" bedroom. And no Roger or Doris or Alice Thumb.

She has noticed Theo's problem with speech. He has scarcely spoken. He lies as if exhausted, his eyes closed.

Zita laughs again, although she is not the kind of person who has laughter to spare and make use of in incongruous moments.

"You catch up with your reading, Theo. All Irving's town planning books and papers. *The Growth of Cities. The Ideal City. Twin Cities.* And the model, you can study the model city."

He does not answer. He has fallen asleep.

Later that evening Dr. Grant tells Zita of Theo's real condition. He explains that there has been a slight "vascular accident" which has affected both his speech and his power to find words for his thoughts.

"It's something we take for granted. Think a thought and a word is there, a phrase, a definition. Like throwing out a line and hooking a fish every time." (Dr. Grant is a keen angler.) "But with this vascular accident, the line is out and baited, and the fish are there, as they've always been, but they no longer take the bait or are aware of its existence; the two worlds have separated."

Dr. Grant does not use the word "stroke" or "cerebral hemorrhage" thereby, in his own way, removing Theo from

206

the dreaded area of disease to the commonplace of having a body subjected to the peculiarities of its own highway traffic. A "vascular accident." Zita finds the language acceptable. After all, she and Theo have lived five years in California and she is aware that, just as in New Zealand, the predominant image is of sheep and cattle, and headlines such as "Stubborn disease conquered," "Prenatal research praised" tend to refer to the study of animals rather than people. So in California the image is of automobiles, their make, their habits and disasters. Doris and Roger are surprised at her calm announcement, "Theo has had a vascular accident."

Roger, whose uncle has had a stroke, says, "Don't worry. With medicine these days he'll live to be a hundred."

"I wish we didn't have to leave," Zita says. "You know, we have only a few days left. Theo could have convalesced on the patio and watched the deer coming into the garden. We have nothing like that down on Shattuck."

She thinks: "As we knew the Garretts and actually lived in the same city, it's a great shame they didn't leave their house to us. We'd take such care of it. I think we need it. The air up here near Grizzly Peak would be better for Theo. And there's a view. And when you're sick you like a view."

All day, no one has asked Roger about his experience in the desert.

PART FIVE

*Avoiding and Paying Attention to
Keepsakes and Shelter, and the
Withering of a Tongue Blossom.*

33.

Having made my final concession to the historic present in writing about my guests, I emerged from my studio as they were making their preparations to leave. Theo, miraculous Theo, they said, had recovered enough to be spoken of, with prompting from him, as "his old self" although it was clear that his choice of language had become limited and he tended to give definitions rather than nouns or descriptions of actions rather than the name of the action. He had lost much of the power to name — the God-power and poet-power. Roger, who had had time to tell the others of his hours in the desert and so redress the balance of attention, had developed a brotherly friendship with Theo, while Doris and Zita, who were not quite liberated women, had settled together in the hinterland of the city of suffering toward which Theo and Roger turned, dazzled by the bright lights and ready to pay for their accommodation in the currency of desert journey and vascular accident. Theo seldom made the effort to speak now. The agony of the loss of the power to name showed clearly in his eyes, and only Roger appeared to be able to accept Theo's experience as a version of a desert journey. Doris now raised her voice to speak to Theo, as if he were deaf, and even Roger had a new way of gesticulating as if Theo might not understand what was being said to him. And sometimes Theo answered with gestures, like a kind of sign language, reinforcing the feeling that he was becoming inaccessible through words. Zita spoke to him in extra soft tones, for no clear reason except perhaps with the hope that her words, like soft whispers of rain, might be absorbed through his skin, feeding him the lost language.

Among my guests once more, and sharing the facilities of the house, I found myself again troubled by its odd shape, the rhombus rooms, the narrowing rectangle of the bathroom, the sloping wall of the Prestwick's room, although I think I was less troubled by the odd angles than by the reminder that the house had been built according to fashionable theory — why live in boxes like captured beetles, why not live in unsquare, unrectangular rooms; why have fireplaces level with the floor, why not raise them to table level (this accounted for the raised fireplace in the living room, also for the "sunken" garden in the hallway). The house had the charm of its originality and of the strength of conviction of the owners, but it still made me uneasy. I had not been able to work at my novel about the Watercress family and Margaret Rose Hurndell. I had been forced to concentrate on my four guests. I had not even had the satisfaction of telephoning Brian to give the news of my inheritance; it seemed that he was still in Europe, and though it was usual for him to send a postcard or a letter on hotel stationery, I had had no word from him. Soon, however, within a few days, I would be flying back to Baltimore, and New Zealand.

I'd heard so much about the Carltons' tiny apartment down on Shattuck, and their failure to find a new place that suited them, and I might earlier have had the attitude that not having a home was "their own fault," but Theo's condition recalling that of Lewis Barwell, my first husband, aroused my sympathy and I thought, Why shouldn't I give them the Garretts' house, why shouldn't Theo have the chance of living in a nameless street beneath a nameless peak, and look out over the nameless city and the nameless

Bay? I dearly wanted the house and its contents, as some-one may want two coats "in case" or *three* coats or stereos or TVs or bank accounts or professions or life-partners. There are some who live entirely "just in case," expecting disaster and needing the material armor to face it; and they are related to those who live entirely through the dream of alternative choices, expecting pleasure and satisfaction. I am neither one nor the other. Also, I did not wish to give up my home in Stratford, Taranaki, New Zealand, a small noisy town with the inevitable rose garden, clock tower, and scout den; and the streets named after Shakespearian characters. I still hope to find silence to write in this town of motor-mowing, chain-sawing, hammering, stereo-playing, panel-beating citizens. I still have faith in the town because it has a river and Shakespearian names . . .

I decided to give the house to the Carltons.

34.

I woke in the early morning, the day before the guests were to leave. I had arranged my own flight for the following day, when the Garretts would have been returning.

The heatwave had broken. The white flowers, the hummingbirds' favorite had almost finished blooming; I could see clusters of withered petals and smell their scent through the partly open window of my studio. I opened the studio door and looked out at the still-sleeping wooded world — that part of the Berkeleif Hills belongs to the trees, as the fires well know when, from summer to summer they dance their flames from hilltop to hilltop, swallowing hills and valleys and using the trees as chorus to enhance and support their performance. The season was ripe for fire. The long grass was dry, the drought and the heat had lasted for weeks. I sat at the door (remembering Lance, and the Battle of Blenheim, and the house on Bannockburn Road, the distant Waitakeres and the sun setting) and I watched the morning grow. I saw a red fox running by in the road, and a troop of deer moving from garden to garden, for the fashion there was for low fences, or none, for wilderness garden and roadside with herbs, daisies, tall grasses thick with bees and blossom that would have horrified the lawn connoisseurs of New Zealand who can judge a lawn as skillfully as they can judge the gloss of a horse's coat or a sheep's wool, and who, fearful, cannot accept a wilderness garden which would give an invitation to bees, butterflies, birds — and *fire*.

I saw a skunk coming down the steps by the corner of the house, walking sedately step by step, like a woman in a black and white fur coat going to the opera, walking down the stairs of the circle to take her place in the front row. Seen by everyone, with her glossy furs, but possibly wearing a more discreet brand of perfume. I felt the gratitude that I always feel at the sight of creatures of the wild going about their daily affairs undisturbed.

Later, when we were all relaxing on the patio, (by the raised garden) I said, darning a hole in the silence, drawing the thoughts of each of us together, "I saw a skunk this morning, walking down the steps. No," I said in answer to their startled glances and sniffs, "I didn't frighten it."

"There are skunks around here," Theo said. "You have to be careful."

We listened nervously as he spoke, and we were thankful that for once he had not been forced into a panic of circumlocution. He was surprised, too, and smiled jauntily like his "old self."

"I've never seen a skunk," Doris said.

"Yes, there are many in the hills," Zita confirmed, stamping Theo's progress with her words and her smile.

"They're very wise animals," Roger said, and I'm sure we knew that he had just invented this fact. He'd become an expert on the local and desert flora and fauna and clearly wanted to keep his role, but the glib "very wise animals" was too condescending to be true.

Feeling sorry for Roger (I am susceptible to out-of-element men who don't realize they are proclaiming the fact) I let the others know my own terrible limitations by saying, "I've seen skunks before only on TV. And that's how I knew it was a skunk."

There followed heavy, worsted generalities specked with arguments for and against television. The unreal, the real experience. Living, dreaming. Armchair explorers, ornithologists, zoologists; musicians, magicians, rapists, lovers, villains.

"I saw five babies born last week," Zita said.

She turned to Theo, speaking for him as some mothers speak for their children or as the confidently found whole speak for the flawed, the defective.

"Theo and I lived through the life of a white rhinoceros."

"I lived under the sea with whales," Doris said.

"Well," Roger said bravely, "I haven't watched much TV. I saw a hummingbird here in the patio. And when I looked up in the sky the other day I saw hundreds of butterflies, miles away."

"They're migrating," Zita explained, "or coming to their summer home. I forget which. I saw them on TV."

Slowly the hole of silence opened again: a sweet green emptiness that stayed till noon.

After lunch I said grandly to Zita and Theo, "I'm giving you the house. I have my own home in New Zealand and I could never afford the taxes here, nor could I run a car, and you need a car in these hills. At home we have corner groceries and dairies. Here —"

"But Irving and Trinity left it to you . . ."

"Even so —"

"Would you not want to let it, perhaps? You might want to stay here some time in the future."

I could see that Roger and Doris did not approve of my apparent generosity.

"But to give it all away."

They turned to Zita and Theo, "You won't really accept, will you? It will go against the wishes of the dead."

"I think we will accept it." Zita said.

She took Theo by the arm, transmitting the current of acceptance.

"Yes." Theo said.

"We feel that Irving and Trinity would understand." Zita said, attributing to the dead, as the living do, greater powers of understanding and wisdom and forgiveness.

"Yes," Theo said again. "It's very kind of you. I do think they would realize what it means to us."

He was outside the boundary: not a noun in sight. Pronouns, yes, but they are mere replicas, stand-ins, shadows.

"I think they would, too." I said. "They left the house to me solely on the strength of one meeting, and the reading of my two books, especially *The Green Fuse*."

"Which was that?" Zita asked, trying to sound as if she had read it and knowing that I knew she hadn't.

"The one about life in a mental hospital."

"Oh, yes," Roger said. "It shook them."

"Why, especially?" Doris asked.

Evidently they did not know of the wolf-child, Adelaide, and I did not enlighten them. I felt her presence then, and that of the twins I had known; I have given up trying to escape from them. The Garrett child crouched in the corner of the sitting room where we'd gathered to discuss the choice of keepsakes. I could hear her whimpering and now and again she howled, like a wolf, and made the sounds but not the shape of human speech.

"Yes," I said, trying to appear calm. "the Garretts would approve of your having the house. Their intentions were good, and it's marvelous to have a place like this if you can afford it. As you know I'm returning to Baltimore the day after tomorrow and then flying home."

"But you won't regret giving it all away like this? It does belong to you. And it's a *dwelling-place*."

That was Zita, put into doubt by the English language, speaking the word "dwelling-place" as one who had learned English and still used some formal words that appear only in books and legal documents, and who as once an officially Displaced Person could feel the full meaning of the word and its history, knowing or sensing the derivation—the old

217

Teutonic gedwolen, gone astray, the Old Sanskrit dhwr, dhur, to mislead, deceive, stun, stupefy, to hinder, delay, tarry — and abide, remain.

"I already have somewhere to live," I said sharply knowing that I did hate to give the house away. But what could I do?

"What would you like to take with you?" I asked the Prestwicks, adding that Julian Soule was arranging for most of the books to be crated and sent to New Zealand.

"One hasn't much choice, with air travel," Doris said. "Will it seem strange to take that wooden mask of Shakespeare?"

"Don't hesitate." I said generously. "Anything you wish. The cloth hangings, the pre-Columbian pottery. . . ."

It occurred to me that Doris and Roger might be hesitant to choose through some mistaken idea that their choice might expose them to each other, for they appeared to be taking special care to crystallize the more fluid aspects of their personalities—the result could have been permanent jewels or temporary icicles, I was not to know which. I knew only that Roger seemed determined to emerge as "spiritual" and Doris as "practical, earthy."

"We both thought it was a good idea to take the Shakespeare mask," Roger said.

Of course. The expected decision.

"Also—"

"Yes?"

"The Persian carpet in the hallway. And Doris has something else haven't you dear?"

"The golden blanket," Doris said quickly. You know the one. We've all admired it."

I heard Zita gasp as if something had touched an exposed nerve. And I felt dismay. I had wanted the golden blanket. I knew that I could still have it, as everything belonged to me, but to make an issue of it would be to reveal myself when I, too, had taken care to fix the view of myself which others might see.

"The golden blanket is more or less part of the household linen." I said casually. "And I had intended to take the linen. Would you prefer a tapestry? Or one of the magnificent art books? Or that book about the desert?"

"Well," Doris said slowly. "I know Roger would like the book on the desert, wouldn't you?"

She went over to the bookcase by the piano where the outsized books were kept, and found *The Desert*. We watched her. I saw in each face the unhappy greed of those who cannot live by bread alone or soul-food but need carpets and furniture and blankets.

Blankets.

I said lightly, "Yes, I will take the linen and blankets. As an example of bedding in the United States."

An acceptably colonial explanation, I thought. In an age of explanation one can always choose varieties of truth.

Doris was tenacious.

"The blanket would be light to take by air . . . Also there are some lovely little pots and jars in the kitchen. I thought I might have some of those. You did say choose anything."

I nodded.

"Oh."

Zita's dismay was apparent. "Not that lovely blue ginger jar."

"I was thinking exactly of that."

"Oh no, please!"

They both looked at me. I was the owner, wasn't I? Zita's *please* had behind it all the force and distress of a displaced person whom the blue ginger jar would place at once, in her own *dwelling-place*, Grizzly Peak Road, Berkeley Hills.

"As Zita and Theo are going to live here, perhaps they can have the ginger jar. But decide among yourselves. There are many other objects — that painting in the hall-way."

"Texture Three?"

"Yes."

Nobody wanted the painting in the hallway.

219

It was the usual story. Only the still subduing heat of the day prevented us from climbing to pinnacles of intensity and crying out our choice of the Garretts' remains, one after the other, fighting for possession of our claims. It could have been any death of anyone, linked by blood, and passionately loved and mourned: it was only the Garretts.

Only the Garrets.

We had given them so little time in our thoughts and our conversation and if any of us had prayed it might have been, as usual, for the ease and forgiveness of our own lives and not for the scarcely known dead. I thought of the Garretts' memorial service, the eulogy given by the retired professor of town planning, who also lived in the Berkeley Hills and who also had reserved his place in Carmel. I thought of the Irving's model city displayed in the funeral home, and the way the funeral director had touched it up with gold paint and rested it on a purple velvet cloth draped over a simple deal table. The Garretts had specified in their will a *deal* coffin and Julian Soule had thought that in the circumstances a deal table would account for their wishes. A *deal* table. I wondered where the Garretts had found and kept the word "deal"—perhaps it was one of those long lost words of English which emerge in isolated parts of North America and make one believe one is living in a past age. Or perhaps the Garretts had found the word where I found it— I suddenly felt the shivering ache of being in touch with fiction, a world at once vanished and newly imagined: Jane Austen, George Eliot, the Brontës; and all the deal tables that in memory were part of the furniture of the old houses —in the kitchen at Wuthering Heights, in the dining room at Lowwood school, the school at Brussels; the Mill on the Floss; the houses of Dickens. I felt then like breaking down and weeping.

We finished our arrangements. The blankets and linen were to be sent to me in New Zealand. The books too, the

Yeatsless collection. Julian Soule (for his enormous fee which could readily be paid from the estate, leaving me, to my delight, a small yearly income) would arrange the mailing, and would even send any furniture I might want to keep. How hard it was to decide! My first thought was to take the study desk but it did seem both impractical and greedy to ship it home when I already have the desk once used by the editor of Landfall, although it and I are not always on good terms.

I was glad when night came. We were all exhausted and even before I fell asleep my mind was in the midst of dwelling-places and furniture and I think I must have dreamed, waking and sleeping, of all the houses I had lived in and all the blankets that had warmed me.

35.

Oh there were empty houses and houses half-constructed where, as children, we stamped about on the bare winter-pale wood sending up a cloud of sawdust into the half-formed rooms, where the wall-frames rose up like thin unfleshed arms and the roof was partly sky, summer-blue, endless as our vision of childhood and life without death. There were houses surrounded by trees and houses without trees, and houses within trees; with swamps and red-weeded ponds and lank grasses crowned and veiled by the eternal spider-houses with their tenuous, swinging, sparkling stairways leading from door to door across the air; for the spiders and the beetles and the birds also looked for shelter and hiding-place; and even the blood in our bodies had its own secret cell where the structure of its life could be cherished in health and preyed upon, destroyed, in sickness; and whatever happened to the blood-cell happened also to the houses, in a different form with a different name—in the strewn beetle legs and the stray bird feather and in the spilled blood, seen or unseen, in the curtained human house.

All night I dreamed of those houses—the early places by the railway line, by the railway goodshed or the engine shed, the tall macrocarpas, the piled sacks of grain with their stuffy dusty smell, the railway color of the paint on the railway huts, the trucks, the sheds, the house roofs; and all the other houses, unrailway, with yellow banksia roses and a deep yellowed bath and big high-ceilinged rooms with the piles of borer-dust along the floor by the skirting boards and in the corners and behind the door and the mirrored wardrobe; and then the formal houses, those of other people, full of fear and strangeness and foreign order, with hostile other-smelling furniture and level undented beds and crocheted doilies and fringed blinds; and lace; and china, blue china cups and saucers that let in a faint blue light which shone on the faces of the adult tea-drinkers, the aunts, cousins, neighbors, giving their skin a blue sheen, like celluloid: artificial, inflammable; with eyes chipped, in glass molds; the terrible strangers in the best-behavior holiday houses stacked and stocked with *pleases* and *thank yous* with a small heap of *may I's* and *pardon me's* packed among the few layers of threadbare hand-me-downs in the holiday suitcase, the family suitcase lined with a silk that was called "shot" silk — grey, streaked with its own blood.

I dreamed of my first formal house, my foreign cushioned carpeted bed-sitting room in the home of Mrs. Tomlin in Maori Hill, Dunedin; Mrs. Tomlin who each year "took in" a student boarder and whose life was overflowing with her married daughter and her grandchildren, and who spent most of her time with them in the new government estate over the hill. Lorna and Tom and the children. She never tired of talking about them. She'd be up early in the morning with her coat and hat on, ready to go "over the hill" to Lorna's place, and every evening at the dinner table that was always crowded with plates and little dishes and china boats and bowls, with mounds of moist food streaming like small volcanoes, she'd talk of the day at Lorna's, a detailed account from moment to moment.

My room was dark with a polished floor and a window so modestly and carefully dressed that a glimpse of light rarely showed except when I cautiously sprang the brown fringed blind up a few inches. Once or twice when it rushed up the full length of the window, a rectangular block of light came hurtling in, striking the dressing table and the carpet and the polished floor and the bed and the slippery rose colored bedspread with a blow that threatened to rob them of all color in the sun-suffering process known as "fading." Then I hastily retrieved the blindcord and shut out the sun.

"Keep the curtains drawn and the blinds down; it's the only defense," Mrs. Tomlin said. "I've seen some shocking examples of fading."

Her one complaint about Lorna was that she allowed all her furnishings to fade.

"And I trained her so well!"

I dreamed, too, of the hospital cells with the small high-up, barred and shuttered window, and the door that had no inside handle, and I recalled my feeling of horror each time I touched the door and found nothing to grasp. Have you ever lived in a room where the door has no handle on the inside, where the bed is a straw mattress on the floor, the blanket a square of grey canvas, and the chamber pot a stinking licorice-black rubber vessel, grey at the rim where the urine has aged it, where the walls are stained and scarred, where they have been beaten and thumped and kicked by frightened people? They had left their fossilized screams and cries, like a mine, for me to explore, and in one corner, though you could not see it unless you found the right focus, there was a mountain of salt formed through the many seasons of many tears, and all over the walls and ceiling and the floor, the oval shape of the peephole-peeping eyes had burned their brand. Those cells were cells of despair. They were the last place to be: after that, there was nowhere; they were the rehearsals of death while the thousand eyes were the steady uncaring eyes of grass blades and sun-filled daisies and marigolds, the burr marigolds, the tickseed sunflowers that leave the stain of their touch only on the living. Made warm by them, what do the living care about death? After all, the sun returns each day to the sky, the promise of morning is kept, in spite of cathedral arguments, the stony-faced insistences about the identity of the originator of the promise.

You see, I was carried away in my dream, as one may be. And I dreamed of other dwelling-places, in my first journey away from New Zealand after Lewis died and I traveled through the Spanish islands and knew the earth and flowers and creatures that surround the houses: that snow-smelling bedroom in the Pyrenees with the big featherbed; and the slices of snow wedged in the window; the almond and beanflower-smelling rooms in the islands where the windows overlook the sea and the sand, and the dry homeless tumbleweed roams across the beach, curled upon itself, blown over and over in the wind; and the salt marshes burn with blue flowers.

And I dreamed of the house on the island in the Bahamas with the furry rats on my pillow, and the scorpions on the floor and the diamond-backed rattle of the coconut palms in the night wind; of the marigold-smelling Flint Cottages of Norfolk; and the cabbage- and varnish-smelling bedsitter in London where my daughter Edith lived until she found her flat; the soot-smelling rooms that were "home," the plastic slop and water buckets, the whistling kettles, the gas rings with the gas lingering at every joint, crevice, around the gas pipe, beneath the windowsill, and in the tenants too, in their joints and crevices, at their fingertips, on their skin, while their hearts must have surrendered their power of beating to the city traffic which, like a giant pacemaker, took over heart-duty, while the actual heart remained in its role of a tired bedsitter muscle, kin at last with the metal gas ring, the frayed linen, the thread-bleeding carpet and the chipped cold-water sink on the landing.

I dreamed of all the houses and homes and nests of the world's real and unreal estate; the originals, the replicas; and even of the wheelbarrow home which I saw in the shelter of a London bank, closed for the weekend, with an old woman and her four cats and two dogs and her bundle of possessions, setting up house for the weekend, the animals without murmur or bark, still as corpses in the wheelbarrow while the old woman, her coat spread beneath her, an old blanket over her, her head pillowed on the bundle of clothing, slept in the sheltered entrance to the bank beneath the poster which said, "Your financial problems solved. Instant housing loans. No fuss no waiting personal attention." The old woman slept, her arm around one of the cats, a mottled grey mangy creature with a bitten left ear and a purr that, rivaling the shudder of the underground trains, nearly shook the foundations of neighboring Kings Cross, St. Pancras, and Euston Stations.

And I thought of the room in Menton in the villa where Margaret Rose Hurndell had lived, and how I had visited the room. I walked up a narrow street beneath a railway bridge and up another street that had once been a Roman Road, and on the left I saw the plaque, *Margaret Rose Hurndell Memorial Room*, giving the date of her birth and death (born 1930—the same year as the Princess Margaret Rose — died in 1957; and like Peter Wallstead largely unknown until after her death) and a list of her writings. The garden was overgrown with weeds, the stairs leading to the small garden were thick with sodden leaves and fragments of paper thrown off the street. I put the Margaret Rose Hurndell Key (which I had borrowed) in the lock and pushed open the sun-blistered wooden door which permitted itself to open halfway: it had "dropped" like an old used womb. I walked in. I opened the tiny windows, pushing back the branches that crowded against them. The room slowly became "aired" like old stored linen. Small chutchutting birds with whistlings and secretive noises began stirring outside. A cool wind blew through the windows and out the door, a between-winter-and-spring wind. There was an air of desolation in the room and beyond it. A water-spotted plaque inside gave further details of Margaret Rose Hurndell's career. There were a few straight-backed vicarage-type chairs in the room, and a desk and a bookshelf (an Armstrong Fellow came each year to work in the memorial room); and layers of cold along the bare, tiled floor. I could hear the grass swaying in the neglected garden, and the brittle rustling of the flax bush, now a mass of soaring green spears, which a sympathetic writer had planted near the crumbling wall.

Here, I thought, if one were a spirt or dead, is a sanctuary. With a sudden rush of wind, dead leaves, twigs and a scrap of paper blew inside. The air of desolation and neglect increased: the chill, of the wind and of the spirit, intensified and there was the kind of peace that one feels walking among the dead and listening, as the dead may, at a great distance from the world and its movement and noise.

I went to explore the small garden and found a green garden seat which I cleared, brushing away the bruised ripe loquats fallen everywhere from the huge loquat tree; and I lay down, half in sun, half in shadow, looking up at the lemon tree in the neighboring garden of the Villa Florita. I closed my eyes. The sun came out again, moving quickly, and was on my face, burning. I changed my position on the seat. The sun was once again hidden behind cloud, the air was chill again, the flax rustled with a brittle snapping sound and the secretive small birds once again began their whispering and chittering. I fell asleep. And when I woke I shivered with cold. The mountains were harsh and grey with fallen used daylight, softened in the crevices with the blue of distance and evening.

So that was the Rose Hurndell Room! I dreamed of it, and of my own home in Bannockburn Road, Blenheim, and the two lives I had known there, and the daily use which marriage makes, one of the other, as the light makes of the twin slopes of the mountain, and I was glad that the color of distance was beginning to touch my view of my life in

Bannockburn Road. I dreamed of Brian's house in Baltimore, and of the front window massed with plants. And of
my home in Stratford, once again near the railway line and
the bracken, with the hay-fever trees, white-blossoming,
growing everywhere, and the light green pine mysteriously
transplanted from some Spanish island, growing in the front
garden. Finally, in that disturbed night when I was partly
awake and partly asleep, I thought of the blankets.

Unlike the deal tables of fiction and the drain-layer and
French master, the debt collector, the inhabitants of
Blenheim, of Baltimore, of Berkeley, and I as other than
Violet Pansy Proudlock, ventriloquist or gossiping Alice
Thumb, a secret-sharer of limited imagining, the blankets
were real, with real history and real power of warming. I
thought of those in my home in New Zealand, gathered
from many places, from our old home in the south, from my
parents' bed — coarse blankets matted with being washed
and almost threadbare in places, faded from white to yellow
with age and sun and hanging year after year on the clothesline, strung between two appletrees, tautened and lifted
into the arms of the wind by the manuka clothes-prop,
returning to sag and swing close to the earth with the weight
of the wetness. Their brand names were marked in the
corners. Some were English—*Wilton*—a name I had heard
spoken with the reverence obviously due to it; others, with
names that caused a shiver of homesickness, a memory of
school days when places became their products —
Onehunga, Mosgiel, Kaiapoi: the places with the woolen
mills and therefore the blankets. I remember my mother
looking out at the fluffy-clouded sky with its patches of pale
blue, saying, "It's blanket weather." That meant washing.
The washing was a remembered ritual and risk. The wom-
en's magazines printed regularly long serious articles with
such titles as, "Dare I Wash My Woolen Blankets?" and
"The Risk of Washing Woolen Blankets," sometimes pages
of "Hints On Washing Woolen Blankets."

Blankets in their washing and drying were part of the poetry of the outside world and its weather.

"the white sheet bleaching on the hedge
with Heigh the sweet birds how they sing"

It seemed that, among all the products of the earth, wool was the most important, especially when our early education dealt largely with products, with the implication that living depended less upon the heartbeat and import and export of breath than upon the import and export of products: wool, butter, mutton. In recent years there was even a prime minister who came from the home of blankets — *Kaiapoi*, and brought, naturally, a new share of warmth and compassion to the nation. How could he help it, coming from *Kaiapoi*?

But the price of wool! The cost of the warmth has always been too great. I know, who live outside fiction where the cold wind blows across the waste spaces from heart to heart.

Finally, I dreamed of the Garretts' golden blanket which everyone had wanted, I knew. I knew just as surely that it was mine, that it would take its place among the other treasured blankets in my home — that grey pair which I bought one week in a silverfish and ant-infested seaside beach in the north, the relic of a cold wet summer, when Lewis was alive, and the children were small, and we all lay shivering in our dripping hammocky beds, and the manuka and the sea outside were full of misty rain. And there was the purple blanket that was returned to me when the writer I met on my first visit to New York died suddenly. I gave it to her after I had stayed in her apartment, but after she moved from there, something happened, she couldn't find enough warmth, though the world was crying out for warmth and wool, and so, they told me, she stayed all day in her new apartment with the curtains drawn, the radio playing the black power station (in the days when black Americans, flying to San Francisco, could still be paged, unthinkingly, to "come to the white courtesy telephone"), and with bottles of tranquilizers and fuming low-calorie sodas ranged along the window-sills. Beatrice, married at sixteen, divorced, a daughter at college. Beatrice, writing her novel, playing her music, perpetually depressed. They found her body in the East River. The purple blanket might have warmed her, but in the end there was no room left in her hibernating, winter heart for further cold seasons. Yes, her purple blanket is now safe at my home in Taranaki, with the other relics of warmth. And soon the gold blanket would be there too, I thought. I'm sure I smiled in my sleep realizing that I had won the gold blanket from the guests; unfairly, perhaps, but the price of warmth is often too high for too close a scrutiny of the means of getting it.

36.

The next day the Carltons returned to their downtown apartment to make arrangements for living in the Garretts' house. The Prestwicks took their flight over the Pole to London where Roger would be planning his "real" visit to the "real" desert. I was relieved to be alone in the house to prepare for my departure the following morning.

In spite of the constant use of the house in the past weeks, everything seemed to be dustier, the rooms had an air of neglect, and even some of the preserves, half-used by the Garretts, were growing mould; the Australian ginger in its golden syrup was specked with grey dots the size of large fullstops. And the birthday candies still lay on the coffee table in the sitting room, and when I saw them, and knew that I had eaten them and disposed of the box, I began to have doubts about the time I'd spent in the house, all those hours working out of sight downstairs attending to the fictional needs of my guests, with the neighbors all away for the summer (my poet friend, too, with her husband away designing yet another Futureland). And although the Prestwicks had flown home to London, the mask of Shakespeare with his gouged eyes and burned forehead, still stared from the wall by the patio door, and the huge book, *The Desert* still lay on the coffee table; and there were the photos of Trinity in her bunny wool cardigan; both the girl, and the woman of nearly seventy, which I believed I had stored with other photos; and the replicas everywhere —the marble table, the sculptures, the paintings and the prints of paintings and the prints of prints of paintings; and still set out on the study table beside the desk, the model city, the centerpiece at the memorial service in the funeral home of the Carmel Retirement Center. I could see, on closer examination, that Irving had already begun his work on redesigning Blenheim, and a typed folder in the desk drawer confirmed this. He had listed the street names. There they were, all the battles and the generals—my own Bannockburn Road, Heavenfield Mall, Malplaquet Place, Hohenlinden Road ("On Linden when the sun was low"), Montgomery Square, Maldon Street ("then clamor rose, ravens wheeled, the eagle greedy for carrion; there was shouting on earth . . ."); Ashdown Street; but all had been changed to fit Irving's dream and only the battle names of the streets remained: parks, gardens, schools, community centers; churches, concert halls, libraries; light-filled houses; nothing less than a heavenly city with the human reminder in the names of the streets, and a small plaque, by the side of the crossroads, to the dead poet.

And in the desk drawer I found a cardboard box full of tiny model people—bought, beautiful people, families to pose at the doors of the houses, model officials, a model church congregation, model shoppers to throng the model streets or sit on the model seats in the model parks beneath a model sun. Only, as far as I could see, there were no model poets.

And the chart, The History of the World and its Peoples, still hung on the wall. Had the Carltons or the Prestwicks wanted it? I had the idea that Doris, with her interest in maps and geography, had claimed it. I noticed, too, that Theo had not taken the book on erosion which he'd said he wanted to consult, but perhaps it did not matter, as they were returning to the house. Yet Doris had taken none of the cookery books she said she wanted.

I decided to clean the house. I put the stale candies and

232

the moldy preserves out in the trashcan, I dusted the furniture and the (Yeatsless) bookshelves and the walls, and I even dusted the model city, the replica of Blenheim, pausing, whimsically, to erase a few specks from Bannockburn Road; and slowly the house began to look less forlorn. I put fresh flowers in the main bedroom and tidied the downstairs study where I'd been working among waves of littered papers that stayed as a fixed tide which I dared not disturb as I worked, for all those seabirds that circle and cry out in the lonely inner skies had settled there. And when the house had been put in order I packed my typewriter and the neglected Watercress novel and a few possessions (including the gold blanket). I telephone Brian in Baltimore to say I'd be there the next day and perhaps would stay a few days before I returned to New Zealand. He was still not home. I could hear the phone ring echoing in the house. His stay in Europe must have been extended—or did he say his visit was to Brazil? I looked forward to my return to Baltimore, and to telling Brian of the Happenings in Berkeley. So settled in his life with his fixed hours of work and his carefully organized routine, he'd be amazed, I thought, to hear all my news: the Garretts' deaths, the inheritance, the guests, when only a few weeks ago my life (and the manifold) had been filled with Brother Coleman, Mrs. Tyndall, the damp unhappy small boy from New Zealand, and the family heirloom which his visit discovered locked for safe keeping in Brian's heart; and the children of the street, and the dead poet of the city. Thinking of Brian and my return, I told myself that I'd sleep this time in the foldaway bed in the sitting room, just below the air conditioner, and I'd leave the basement and its cockroaches and the turning wheels of the traffic and the sensation of lying almost directly beneath them, and the unnerving recognition of having, where a neighboring bedroom would be, a weaving of sewer and gas pipes tenanted by city rats and occasionally, as rumor said, by an alligator.

Then the following day, at noon, I was waiting at the door

37.

Outwardly, I remained calm. When I first heard of the death of the Garretts and the terms of their will, my feeling was of disbelief. Had I known them, I might have turned away from, avoided, the possibility and responsibility of feeling, by going at once to another, a private fictional world. As it was, my disbelief at first, like a thermometer reading, soared to the top of the scale, after which it dropped to a normal usual state, varying from day to day as I tried to realize and accept what had happened. Confronted suddenly by the living Garretts, I again suffered the fever, but there is a quality about presence, people, their bulk and their shadows, their being outside the pages of a book, not anchored by words, which transports one to the shared, unprivate world. The Garretts were alive.

Before I could register any outward feeling, or speak, Irving came toward me, "You've timed it well." he said. "Did you enjoy your stay? Did you get your novel written?"

"You look surprised to see us," Trinity said. "Italy was wonderful. We explored the northern Villages. You must go there, you must. We love Italy!"

My heart was beating very fast, and I knew that my face was pale, and my hands holding the keys were trembling.

"The keys," I said, thrusting the key ring toward Trinity who took it and exclaimed with a childish note of delight, "Oh, look, the Mexican sundial is still on the key ring!"

Well, I thought, what did they expect?

At the same time I understood what it is like to be gone and to imagine that the place you left has vanished or (of a Yeatsian place) has "changed, changed utterly."

"Everything's fine." I said, trying to sound grateful but feeling resentful and still in a state of shock at their arrival. As for my inheritance — how snugly I had nested myself within it!

"And did you get your book written? When will we see it?"

"There were some problems," I said, "but if it gets written and published, I'll send you a copy."

I looked directly at each of them, into their eyes, trying to read again that comforting Last Will and Testament; and remembering Adelaide and the two wolf-children I had known; but there was no sign. I had an impulse to cry out at them, "Tell me, tell me!" But it was no use. I realized that the information was mine, all mine.

"See," I said calmly, pointing to the garden, "I've watered the plants. There's been a drought here, a hot wind blowing from the desert."

I emphasized the word *desert*, half expecting them to talk about Roger and Doris.

Instead they said, "You will promise to send us a copy?"

They laughed together.

"We might be in it!"

I thanked them again for the use of the house, and went to the waiting taxi and as I was leaving I looked out of the window and saw Trinity bending over the pot plants in the raised garden, touching the leaves gently as if touching skin, and I saw Irving, his back to the front door, staring out at the view, the view from home.

They had taken possession.

"There's time." I told the driver. "Go along Shattuck."

I was thinking of Julian Soule and Theo and Zita. I knew exactly where Soule's office was and where Theo and Zita lived, and seeing their place, I thought, would also prove to me that I myself was not just a character out of fiction, a replica of a replica dreaming of a replica of dreams, that I was paying attention and not in the world of total avoidance. I might have known. Certainly, there were young poets in the streets of Berkeley, along Telegraph Avenue, wildly reciting the cherished words, but instead of Julian Soule's office there was a supermarket and a butcher's shop where Theo and Zita had lived.

Feeling apprehensive and confused I boarded flight 28 to Baltimore.

38.

At three that afternoon I arrived at Friendship Airport, took the hotel limousine to the Lord Baltimore Hotel, and from there I persuaded a reluctant taxi driver to take me downtown past the North-East Market to the block where Brian lived on Monument Street. I had my own key and a scrap of paper where I'd written the combination of the front door lock. There was no need to use the keys, however, for as soon as I unlocked the outer door, someone unlocked the inner door and I was face to face with Brian's sister whom I'd met once. She looked pale and very tired.

"I've been wondering about you." she said.

I frowned.

"Yes. The day after you left to go to that house in Berkeley. I sent you a telegram. Didn't you get it? I thought you'd come at once, and then when you didn't come I thought you hadn't been able to face it, that you were avoiding it."

"Avoiding what?" I couldn't remember any important telegram.

"But I sent you the telegram!"

I felt my fear and shock returning.

"The telegram about Brian. He didn't suffer at all. No one knew he was ill."

"But I was here," I said slowly, "winter and spring. Mrs. Tyndall. Lonnie."

"I sent you the telegram," Gloria repeated. Phil and I stayed here to sort things out."

"But I telephoned," I said, seizing facts.

"We must have been out."

"Out? Where would you go?" I asked angrily.

The taxi driver was waiting. I paid him and tipped him the amount he expected for bringing me to an area looked on as "undesirable." I took my suitcases into the sitting room and sat in the big rocking armchair by the golden wire tree. I couldn't speak and I couldn't cry. The permanence of Brian had been unshakeable: a good friend over many years while the vulnerable rest of the world died of their various diseases and accidents, lost limbs and faculties, turned traitor to the wholeness of being alive. And it was partly Brian himself who willed this aura of permanence, for he simply never included death in his plans, thus persuading those around him to exclude it; and he was such an infallible planner! The only time he'd mentioned his own death was when he said he'd given his body for medical research.

Having had beliefs and disbeliefs shaken during the past days I half expected Brain to reappear, as the Garretts had, to prove that once again a fictional banishment, a replica of what might be, but is not, cuts no ice (ice!) with the divine originator. I did not know how I could believe Brian's death, following my experience with the Garretts. When I'd last seen Brian, and after Mrs. Tyndall died, he'd emerged from her death without a trace of it on him, not even a speck as big as the fullstop mold in the ginger jar.

"It was a heart attack," Gloria said suddenly. "One morning. The plumber found him—he had the key and was going to fix a pipe downstairs. Brian was making coffee. He was lying there, in the kitchen."

I've known of other such morning deaths, just at the point of turning to face the new day, of reaffirming life by breaking the night's fast.

I asked Gloria if I might stay overnight, in the small

239

upstairs room, and I phoned the airport to change my flight to the next day. I'd be home in Taranaki in a day or two. There was no reason for me to stay longer in his house. Gloria looked at me curiously when I said, no, no I didn't want a keepsake, and I added, to her, senselessly, "There have been too many keepsakes lately."

"Books? Music?"

"No, no."

I had had enough, in the meantime, of the manifold, and the real and unreal "marble complexities and bitter furies." Of paying attention and avoiding. I reminded myself as I fell asleep that night that, once again, Alice Thumb would take care of everything, in time, that she would direct the glances at or away from according to her judgment of the need, while I, Violet Pansy Proudlock, Barwell, Halleton, Alice Thumb herself, would continue to live and work in the house of replicas, usefully, having all in mind—the original, the other, and the manifold.

JANET FRAME
Faces in the Water

'Like the late Jean Rhys, this remarkable New Zealand novelist
has built up a reputation that fair dazzles, and deservedly so'
Publishers Weekly

Faces in the Water is a novel as wide and deep and unexpected
as...perhaps as madness itself. It is a journey which can be
shared by the reader at many levels, offering the pleasures of
extraordinary writing, insights wrenched from pain and harsh
experience, edges torn from the barriers raised between the
so-called mad and the so-called sane.

Faces in the Water is about confinement in mental
institutions, about the fear the 'sane' have of the 'mad' and the
ways in which that fear transforms into banishment and
punishment of those whose reaction to a truly cruel and insane
world is to move into a world which is self-created.

'I was put in hospital because a great gap opened in the ice floe
between myself and the other people whom I watched...I was
alone on the ice...I was not yet civilised; I traded my safety for
the glass beads of fantasy'

'Janet Frame's evocation of madness is unforgettable...*Faces in
the Water* is especially brilliant in its description of what
happens inside the patient's mind'

Time

'Lyrical, touching and deeply entertaining'
John Mortimer, *The Observer*

Fiction   £2.75